KIN OF THE WOLF

MAGNETIC MAGIC
BOOK 3

LINDSAY BUROKER

1

THE IVORY CASE RESTED ON A BED OF FIR AND PINE NEEDLES, glowing a soft silver under the moonlight trickling down through the evergreens. Carved into its lid, a wolf with its jaws parted, rows of fangs prominent, warned me not to get too close. But why did I *want* to get close?

As I slowly circled the case, damp needles poking at my paw pads, I tried to remember why this had been so important when I'd been in my human form. For some reason, I'd rested the magical artifact here and willed myself to remember to examine it once I became the wolf.

In this form, my senses were keen, and I could see the contours of the case perfectly while smelling the musty scent of its centuries-old ivory. More attuned to magic, I also felt the power radiating from the item. From it and, even more so, from whatever lay within it. An item even more magical and powerful than the case protecting it.

But no great answers came to me. I didn't know what these items did or why they were important. More, I longed to hunt. In my lupine form, the moon called to me, willing me to leave this tiny woodland hemmed in by human dwellings and the noisy vehicle trail beyond the trees. I wanted to run until I reached the forested foothills and the mountains, where I might take down a deer or elk.

So great was the pull that I almost abandoned the case, but I remembered it had value to me in my other form, so I stayed. That didn't keep irritation from ruffling my fur, and when a mouse skittered under the needles nearby, I pounced, snapping it up. Such unsatisfactory prey neither tasted good nor fulfilled my need to hunt. I gnashed on it more out of frustration than desire for the pathetic meal.

With its tail dangling from my jaws, I paused, sensing that I wasn't alone. I turned, peering into the shadows between the trees, and gulped down the rest of the mouse so my fangs would be free if I needed to defend myself.

But this was not an enemy approaching.

A large salt-and-pepper wolf padded into view, heading toward me without fear or wariness. He emanated power, a far more feral and alive kind of power than that of the case, and the moonlight gleamed on his lush fur. I recognized him, a lone wolf who was not from my pack but who'd traveled from a far territory and had helped me on more than one occasion. More than once, we had almost mated.

Duncan was his name in human form, I recalled. And... Drakon. When he'd been called that, I couldn't remember, but I knew it to be true.

When our eyes met, his jaws parted, tongue lolling out, and he bounded forward like a pup rather than a mature male. He lowered on his forelimbs in a playful bow of invitation.

Though we could not speak as humans did, I knew what he wanted. It was an invitation to hunt, to frolic, and to mate.

None of those things sounded unappealing. Again, I desired to abandon the silly human object on the ground.

werewolf, whether I'd been a staunch defender of the complex or not, I would be out of a job. After more than twenty years here, I didn't know what else I would do if they fired me.

Duncan padded along at my side as we approached my apartment. His earlier playfulness had faded, and he looked back into the woods before gazing solemnly at me.

"You think I'm in trouble, don't you?"

He would have gone off to hunt if he hadn't.

His gaze remained solemn.

Yes.

Still in his wolf form, Duncan sat on his haunches, watching me with a cocked head. No doubt, he wanted to know why we hadn't gone off to hunt.

"You can go," I told him as I dressed and put on an oven mitt from my kitchen. With my hand somewhat insulated, I plucked up the case. I could still feel the sizzle of magic, but it was duller through the padding. "Go off and have a good hunt. And thanks for coming out to check on me."

I looked from Duncan to the trees, able to see in the distance the sprawling apartment complex where I lived and was the property manager. Since surviving our confrontation with the *last* people who'd tried to steal the case, Duncan had been staying in his van in the parking lot. Tonight, his nearness had been a good thing.

"I need to put this someplace safe," I added, holding up the case.

Despite being in wolf form, Duncan probably understood me, but he didn't head off to hunt. When I walked toward my apartment, he padded along at my side.

"You're a good..." I groped for the right word. We hadn't had sex and weren't mates, and he'd originally been an enemy, working for my ex-husband to steal the very case I held. I didn't consider him that anymore, but what *was* he to me? A friend? An ally? A future mate? "Wolf," I finished when he looked curiously at me.

Duncan brushed against my side, and I rested a hand on his furred back. It was late enough that none of the tenants were walking their dogs on the grounds, and the lights in most windows were out. I didn't worry too much about being spotted, but I did keep to the trails at the back of the property, avoiding the well-lit areas and the open lawn. I didn't need anyone linking me to the wolves who'd attacked and killed intruders on the property a couple of weeks earlier. If my employers found out that I was a him. Magical energy sizzled against my flesh, both warning and promise of untapped power, but I didn't remove my paw.

Eyes slitted, Augustus looked from Duncan to me and back.

Duncan let his tongue loll out again, a sign of amusement and confidence. He knew we would win if they attacked.

Augustus growled, as much frustration as belligerence. His glare at me was one of loathing. We might be relatives, but that didn't mean he didn't want to kill me. If Duncan had not been there, he would have attacked. I had no doubt.

Instead, Augustus sat back on his haunches and howled. Sending a message to someone? To more cousins? More allies?

I grimaced at the thought. As strong as Duncan and I were, we could only handle so many at once.

Ultimately, Augustus turned, the two other wolves following, and they loped out of the woods. I lowered my paw, relieved when the painful energy the case had spat at it stopped.

Duncan glanced at the artifact, but his gaze locked onto mine, and then he pointed his snout east again. My cousins were gone. Could we go hunt now?

I let out a lupine sigh of dissatisfaction, certain that I needed to stay and guard the case. I doubted my cousins had gone far. If we left, they would pounce on the prize.

Though it was difficult, since I hadn't run through the wilds or known the pleasure of a hunt, I willed the wolf magic to leave my body, for the moon's call to go unheeded tonight. Later, I promised myself as the change came over me, I would go hunt.

Soon, I knelt on hands and knees in the needles, my flesh naked and furless, and the nippy early-December air made me shiver. My human knowledge and memories returned to me as I rose, and I remembered the importance of the case, that a vision had told me it could help my pack—maybe even werewolves everywhere—if I could figure out its secrets. I also remembered that my clothes dangled from a nearby branch.

Duncan pointed his snout toward the east, the unpopulated hunting lands, as if to lead me away, but then his head snapped about. He lifted it into the air, nostrils flaring. He'd caught the scent of something, something dangerous.

As he stood, hackles raised and tail stiff, I also detected it. Another wolf—no, *several* wolves—approached. I sensed their magical auras before I caught their scents. They were familiar but not friendly. Of the pack but not aligned. My cousins.

A dark-gray wolf, a light-gray wolf with a black-tipped tail, and a brown, gray, and white wolf padded side-by-side out of the woods. Their heads were up, their eyes aloof. They looked at Duncan, at me, and at the glowing case.

The eyes of the dark-gray wolf—Augustus—filled with avarice when they locked onto the artifact. He crouched, as if he meant to rush forward and snatch it out from under me.

I growled, prepared to defend it, even from my own pack. *Especially* from my own pack.

The light-gray wolf bumped a shoulder against Augustus and pointed his snout at Duncan.

Duncan was watching them as closely as I, and he loped over to stand beside me, facing my cousins. He also growled, his message clear. He would defend me.

The three wolves eyed us like they might have a powerful moose with deadly antlers. They were weighing the odds. Though they outnumbered us, we were stronger, and they knew it.

Again, Augustus's brown eyes fastened on the box, and I knew what he was thinking. That he might send the other wolves to fight us while he sneaked in like a weasel and stole it. His allies might be maimed or even die to our fangs, but he would have his prize. Why he wanted the silly human thing, I had no idea, but he would *not* get the best of me.

Growling again, I placed my paw on the case and glared at

2

THE NEXT MORNING, WHEN I WANDERED OUT OF MY BEDROOM IN MY robe, I had coffee on my mind, but I spotted a very naked Duncan Calderwood sprawled on my couch and stopped to stare. The night before, I hadn't exactly *invited* him in, but when I'd opened the door, he'd padded inside and lain on the floor, as if to say he would guard the threshold while I slept. With my cousins lurking in the area, possibly plotting ways to attack me and steal the case, I hadn't objected, but he'd been a wolf when I went to bed.

Now, he lay on his back with his arm flung over his eyes and his entire nude body on display.

Though he was a few years older than me—fifty, he'd admitted once—he was as fit as a twenty-year-old pro athlete. The appeal of his muscled form made my gaze linger, despite a notion that I ought to respect his modesty—not that I'd noticed he had any—and drape a blanket over him. Instead, I eyed his powerful frame and the scars the years had left on him, including shackle-like bands around his wrists, and wondered how the night might have ended if we had gone off to hunt together. When our lupine magic waned, we might have ended up in a bed of ferns, enjoying each other's company.

Duncan must have woken and sensed me near because he lowered his arm and looked at me.

The heat of embarrassment flushed my cheeks as I jerked my gaze from his chest—and possibly lower parts.

A smug smile stretched his face. Yes, he'd caught me looking.

"You got fur all over my couch," I blurted, the first thing that came to mind, born out of a silly need to deny that I'd been admiring him. And *wanting* him. He was already full of himself. He didn't need to know those things.

"Did I?" Duncan rolled onto his shoulder, giving me the view of the butt side, and perused the cushions. He plucked a gray strand of wolf fur out of a crack. It wasn't the only one. "Maybe I should have strewn paper towels over the cushions." He'd done that before when I'd warned him not to get blood on the couch. "That would have been hard to do with only paws and teeth though."

I propped a fist on my hip. "I thought you were going to sleep on the floor."

"There was a draft."

"A draft? Wolves in the wild curl up in balls and sleep under mounds of snow."

"Snow is insulating. Those fake wood planks shoot icicles straight through your pelt and into your flanks."

"You must be insufficiently furred if your *flanks* feel the chill from the floor."

Duncan flopped onto his back again and gazed at me with a lot of fondness considering I was insulting him. And was he checking me out?

My robe reached to my knees and was far too fluffy to be sexy, but I hadn't cinched it that tightly... I lifted a hand, thinking of covering more of my chest, but a part of me was chuffed to have him interested. At forty-five, with two grown sons, it wasn't as if I was the ravishing beauty of my youth. Instead, I tossed him a blanket.

"My fur is sufficient," Duncan said. "*All* of me is sufficient."

"Uh-huh. Why don't you cover some of that *all of you*? Where are your clothes?"

"In my van."

"Haven't I had that towed yet?"

He grinned. "You're at your snarky crabbiest first thing in the morning, aren't you?"

As if I couldn't be snarky and crabby at any hour of the day. But I took a breath and attempted to lower my hackles. I wasn't mad at him, just flustered that he'd caught me staring at his brazen nudity.

"I didn't get to hunt last night due to my turds of relatives showing up," I said. "That makes a werewolf crabby."

"Quite true. Though I did spot you with a mouse tail dangling from your lips. You hunted *something*." A twitch of his nostrils was the only indication that he believed it had been substandard prey.

"It was a frustration mouse." I pointed toward the kitchen, specifically at the espresso maker on the counter. "Do you want coffee?"

"Yes, but allow me to make it for you." Ignoring the blanket I'd tossed him, Duncan rose and swept past to beat me to the kitchen. "It's the least I can do after leaving fur on your couch."

Afraid he would mess up my settings or break something, I grabbed his blanket and hurried to bump him to the side. "You can heat up leftovers if you want to be helpful. Or go get clothes and dress before tenants are all over the walkways with their dogs and able to witness and complain about a naked man roaming the premises."

I looked at the windows. The days were short enough this time of year that it wasn't light yet at seven, but it wouldn't be long before the dedicated dog walkers took to the paths.

Duncan touched his chest. "You think they'd *complain*?"

"Yes. There's a no-nudity policy here." I wrapped the blanket around his waist and tied it, giving him a makeshift skirt.

"America is repressed."

"We know. That's how we like it." I poured coffee beans into the hopper.

"I'm pleased to see that you haven't thrown away the gift I gave you." Duncan pointed to a corner of the living room where I'd leaned the antique sword he'd delivered. He'd also given me two months' worth of chocolates after the incident when the scientist, Lord Abrams, had used a magical device to control him and make him attack me.

"Who would throw away a valuable antique sword?"

One that, at least according to him, had silver mixed into the alloy so that it was extra effective against werewolves.

"A woman peeved with a man over a betrayal."

"The betrayal wasn't your fault. *This* time." I gave him a pointed look. By now, I'd forgiven him for taking the thieving gig from my ex-husband, but there was no reason to let him know that.

"I fought the control as hard as I could," Duncan said, his face serious now.

"I know."

He'd sent me flying a couple of times, but I remembered his hesitation, his tormented eyes as he'd fought the magical compulsion. He could have killed me that night, and he hadn't. He'd let me escape. Which was probably why he'd ended up half-dead in a literal ditch.

Duncan looked away, his expression troubled, then took a breath and changed the subject. "Do you know why your cousins are after that case? I thought they only wanted the medallion your mother is set on leaving to you in her will."

I shook my head. "I didn't think they knew about it, honestly. As far as I know, that business guy, Radomir, and your Lord Abrams were the ones behind stealing it."

"He's not *my* lord. Trust me." Duncan peeked into cupboards and removed coffee mugs and plates as we spoke. "I thought he was long dead."

"Rude of him to randomly show up thirty years later with the means to control you."

"*I* thought so."

"I still don't know why he dumped you in a ditch. You're valuable, aren't you?"

"I think his minions were responsible for the dumping," Duncan said without answering the question.

When he'd first reappeared, it had crossed my mind that Abrams had let Duncan go so that he would return to me and, when Abrams activated that magical device again, be close enough to get the artifacts back from me. The case, at least. I'd returned my mom's medallion to her.

"Technically, they may have been Radomir's minions," he said. "I didn't figure out which one of them was in charge."

"They seemed like a team."

"An odd team, yes." Duncan looked in the fridge.

"To answer your question, I don't know why Augustus would want the case. He might have come to kick my ass, and I happened to be studying it when he arrived."

Except that he'd looked at it very intently. And with avarice in his eyes. An odd emotion for a wolf, even a werewolf. I couldn't deny that our human halves were integrated into our being and made us different from non-magical animals, but we weren't our normal selves when in wolf form.

"Did you mean to do that?" Duncan asked. "Study it as a wolf?"

"Yes. I had a hunch doing so might reveal something."

I hadn't told him about the vision I'd had weeks earlier, that I would be able to see and sense more about the case if I looked at it while in my wolf form. It hadn't been until last night, with the full moon creeping closer, that I'd been able to change in a quiet moment when I wasn't threatened or angry or protective. Usually, it took strong animalistic emotions or the moon's power to allow the wolf to come out.

I'd hoped to see much more—to understand more—about the case. Seeing it glow had been vaguely interesting, but it hadn't enlightened me.

I would have to return the artifact to Bolin, my intern and a fledgling druid, to study. To study and to protect from thieving cousins. His father had a safe, and I doubted anyone in my pack knew where his parents lived.

"Did you learn anything from your scrutiny?" Duncan asked, peering into the fridge. "And when you said *leftovers*, did you mean this tub of Greek yogurt? Or these three slices of cheese?"

"I guess I haven't shopped for a while. There's bacon we can cook though. I *know* your carnivorous werewolf genes won't mind that."

"Ah, yes. I do love American bacon. Even when it isn't smothered in chocolate. There aren't, by chance, any of your bars in here, are there?" He looked into the dairy bin.

"No. You store chocolate at room temperature, not the fridge." I opened the cupboard to show him my stash. "As to the rest... I saw the case glow, but that's it."

"I also noticed it glow and felt its power. A *lot* of power. What did you say the inscription translates to?"

Having read the words enough times to have them memorized, I recited, "*Straight from the source lies within protection from venom, poison, and the bite of the werewolf.*"

"It sounds like it's something to thwart our kind, not help them."

"I thought learning about it might reveal something about the lost bite magic."

Duncan looked at me.

"The *mostly* lost bite magic." I arched my eyebrows.

When he'd first told me his story about magically being created in a lab by Abrams, who'd used DNA gathered from a long-dead werewolf found frozen and preserved under a glacier, I hadn't entirely believed it. Since then, I'd witnessed him change into the bipedfuris, the powerful two-legged form that had been lost to werewolves for generations. It was as the bipedfuris that one could bite a human and transmit the magic of our kind.

When Duncan didn't respond, I shrugged. "My mom has lamented that our people have lost that power, that there's not as much magic in the world or in werewolves as there used to be. Since the bite can't create new werewolves, we are, like other magical beings from times past, dying as a species."

"I don't know if that can be changed. It sounds like the case, or whatever is in it, protects people by *undoing* a werewolf bite."

"I know. I just... have a hunch." I took a frying pan out of a cabinet and set it on the stovetop for him. "Do you want black coffee—an Americano?—or a latte?"

"Un café allongé."

"Black, it is."

As I pulled shots, inhaling the scintillating coffee aroma, I debated my hunch and if I had any evidence for it. Other than the wolf on the lid and the mention of bites in the inscription, nothing indicated the case should have significant meaning for our kind. And Duncan was right. The words implied that the artifact would be for staving off werewolves rather than returning their magic to them. Was I grasping at straws? And, if so, why?

"I think I need a mission, Duncan," I admitted as I set his Americano on the counter next to him.

He was peeling off strips of bacon and laying them in the pan. "A mission? I have just the thing."

"Does it involve magnets or magic detectors?"

"Of *course*." Duncan looked at me as if I would be foolish to believe otherwise. "I've been eyeing a fascinating little oasis by a convenience store a few blocks away. There's a boardwalk halfway around a pond with a dock that sticks out into it. Further, there's a cement post thrusting up out of the water on one side, the top sheared off, an ode to a mysterious past era."

"Are you talking about that scummy pond where kids feed the ducks? I think that post had a bat house on it at one point."

"There could be all manner of treasures sunken into the muddy depths under the murky surface." Duncan spread his arms with enthusiasm for this idea.

"Judging by all the loaves of bread that go down duck gullets, there's a lot of poop in the muddy depths."

"The pond calls to me."

"You're a weirdo, Duncan."

"As we've established. But if you don't find fulfillment in replacing faucets and toting toilets around this hive of humanity, perhaps you are correct in seeking a quest."

"The toilets aren't *un*fulfilling. I like taking care of the people here. But the maintenance problems here aren't that challenging to me."

Not mentally stimulating. Maybe that was the right term.

"It's likely a boon for your dwellers if the toilets are unchallenging," Duncan said.

"I think they prefer them that way, yes."

"Is this all you have?" He held up the last strip of the pound of bacon he'd already crammed into the pan. It wasn't going to cook evenly. "I assume you'll want some. A werewolf can't subsist on dairy products alone. That's not even enterically wise for our kind."

"Uh-huh. Bacon is expensive. You're only supposed to eat a few slices at a time." I waved to the fridge. "There are some eggs in the bottom drawer. And what I meant about needing a mission is that... Oh, I don't know. Now that my boys have moved out and are more or less self-sufficient, I feel... I don't know. I used to have to take care of them, and I was on a mission to mold them into decent human beings without the awful tendencies of their father. Now... I'm not sure what I'm supposed to do, other than keeping bad guys from vandalizing cars in the parking lot and shooting up the complex."

"Those seem like quite noble goals."

"And more stimulating than poking through duck droppings for treasures, I suppose." I emptied the portafilter basket and ground more beans.

"Oh, I beg to differ. With as much foot traffic as that pond sees, we're bound to find something good. It's the weekend, is it not? You don't need to work here today, do you? You could come with me."

"I... always have work here that I can do, and I have to be on-call for emergencies, but the leasing office will be closed."

Duncan gazed at me. "I don't know if you answered my question or not."

"I know." I pressed the button to make another Americano.

"Since I don't have any children—probably—" His brow furrowed as he seemed to reconsider that statement before shrugging and continuing. "I can't say that I've exactly experienced what you're going through, but it makes sense that enjoying motherhood and its duties fulfilled you."

"Enjoying isn't quite the word I would use."

He *definitely* hadn't experienced parenthood.

Duncan waved away the comment and continued. "It's natural

that you would seek fulfillment in another vein. And the puzzle of this wolf case has been placed in your lap. Why *wouldn't* you want to solve that mystery? Maybe you were *meant* to solve it." He pushed the bacon around to make room for a ridiculous number of eggs, emptying the carton that should have lasted another week. It was like having teenagers in the apartment all over again. "Perhaps it isn't that you found the case but that the case found you."

"*You're* the one who found it. By waving your magic detector all over my apartment without asking permission."

"That is true, but you should feel vastly grateful for my intervention. Now you've a fascinating artifact to research." Duncan found tongs in a drawer, extracted a lopsidedly cooked piece of bacon from the pan, and offered it to me. "You're welcome."

"That's half raw. You're a better pitmaster than short-order cook."

"A touch of rawness can't bother you. It's not like that mouse you chomped down last night was fricasséed."

"Touché." I accepted the bacon.

"You were cute with the tail dangling out of your mouth."

"An observation that nobody in the world but a werewolf would make."

"The constant struggle, conflict, and risk inherent in our lives teaches us to appreciate what others can't."

"Like mouse tails."

"Cutely *dangling* mouse tails."

Duncan smiled again, the easy handsome smile that always drew me, whether I should let myself be attracted to him or not. With Abrams and his Duncan-control device out there somewhere, keeping my distance seemed wise.

"I was hoping you'd invite me into your bedroom last night," he murmured, unaware of my thoughts.

"So you could get fur on my sheets too?"

"I could have changed first." Duncan patted his flat stomach and waggled his eyebrows. "And then... I could have given you the adventure of a lifetime."

I sipped coffee from my mug. "Given what you consider an adventure, I'm not sure how enticed I should be."

"I *promise* you there's something good in that pond."

Someone knocked at my front door. I didn't know whether to be relieved or disappointed. Whether I should be drawn to him or not, Duncan was good company and easy to spend time with.

"I guess that answers my question about whether you need to work today," he said as I tightened my robe and went to answer the door.

It had grown light out, meaning the hour when Duncan could travel naked to the parking lot without garnering notice had passed. Oh well. I'd knotted the blanket well.

Bolin stood on the threshold, a newspaper tucked under his arm, a whipped-cream-covered mocha in his hand, and bags under his eyes.

"I haven't given you the case back," I said, surprised to see him on a Saturday, "so I know you weren't up late researching it."

"No, I was playing *DWS—Destiny Wields a Sword*. It's a new MMORPG."

"An Em-what?"

"A computer game. You slay vampires."

"Hang around here at night, and you can slay werewolves."

Bolin opened his mouth, closed it, then opened it again. "A month ago, I would have thought that was a joke."

"Sorry." We hadn't yet discussed that I was a werewolf, less because I worried about him sharing the secret and more because he'd started his internship here not believing in werewolves. It wasn't my duty to disavow a youth of his childhood fancies. "If it helps, a month ago, I didn't know druids still existed in the world."

"Really?"

"Well, no. I was aware of the witches, warlocks, and clairvoy-ants in the area, and assumed some druids might be spattered in, but I didn't know any of the ones that existed were allowed to swill coffee, carry man purses, and drive monstrous, gas-guzzling SUVs."

He mouthed the term *man purses*, reminding me that I'd only *thought* that about his expensive leather bag, not voiced the words aloud. But it was the SUV comment that he took offense to. "There's nothing in any druid tenets anywhere that forbids driving a nice car."

"Uh-huh. Are the birds still pooping on it?"

He squinted at me.

"I *know* the plastic scarecrow owls didn't deter them. I saw them abandoned in the maintenance shed with droppings all over them." What did it say about my life that droppings had come up more than once already that morning? That I was close to nature? Or that I was even weirder than Duncan?

"The plastic bubble is working when I take the time to put it up." Bolin shook his head. "I can't believe I came here at the crack of dawn to bring you a newspaper."

"I can't either." I kept myself from adding I was surprised he knew where to buy a physical newspaper—to think, he'd called *me* a Boomer, even though I was barely Gen-X. I'd teased him enough for the morning though. One had to keep up the morale of one's interns, not torment them needlessly. "I assume there's something pertinent in it?"

He held a section from the *Seattle Times* out to me, a photo of the apartment complex, Sylvan Serenity Housing, on the front of the NW section. I slumped against the door frame, certain this didn't herald anything good.

3

THE TITLE FOR THE ARTICLE UNDER THE PHOTO OF THE APARTMENT complex was "Ghost Dogs Feature in Speculation on Sylvan Serenity Murders."

I pushed my hand through my hair. This wasn't the first article that had been printed in the aftermath of the deaths of the thugs who'd driven down here in Teslas, shooting rifles out the windows in an attempt to kidnap me and kill Duncan. *Murders* was a strong word for their fate since the killings had all been in self-defense. The choice worried me. Previously, the deaths had been labeled as freak animal attacks, with nobody implicated. No *humans*, anyway. Since the authorities didn't acknowledge the existence of werewolves, they hadn't brought them up, at least not that I'd heard. I didn't know what Bolin had told the police when they'd questioned him, but I doubted he'd mentioned werewolves either.

"Ghost dogs?" I asked. "That's worse than the article about lions." That had been published the week before. "Where are people coming up with this stuff? There's no evidence to support lions or ghosts."

Maybe I should have been pleased the hypotheses were off the mark—what would I have done if an article had called out *were-wolves*?—but I mostly wanted all discussion of the apartment-complex deaths to disappear. Weren't there other more recent crimes the journalists could write about?

Bolin shrugged. "People don't like unsolved mysteries. They need explanations. One of my professors liked to say that in the absence of facts, we will make up stories to explain things that allow our world views to make sense. Sometimes in the presence of facts too."

"I guess. Well, this doesn't really change anything, right? It's just more speculation. Implausible speculation."

Something about Bolin's expression warned me that I was wrong, that it *did* change something.

"My parents saw the article," he said grimly.

"Oh." As the ramifications of that came to me, I repeated a softer, "Oh. Had they, uhm, not seen the earlier ones?"

"They've been out of the country. I told them there'd been an incident on the premises, but I didn't go into all the details over the phone. I don't *know* all the details since I wasn't there for it. I mostly pointed out that crime has been on the rise in the area."

That was true, and not all of it had to do with me. I was fairly certain the motorcycle gang that had come through in November hadn't been my fault. The riders hadn't been paranormal in any way, and they'd vandalized the parking lot before I'd uncovered the magical case or reconnected with my werewolf family.

The rest of the "crime" around the complex, however, had been my fault. Maybe in a roundabout way, but it had only happened because I lived here. My cousins and Radomir and Lord Abrams had all been after me for one reason or another.

"My parents might come by to talk to you later," Bolin said. "They didn't say when."

That prompted my third, "Oh."

Over the twenty-odd years that I'd worked as the property

manager and, less officially, handywoman, I'd rarely interacted with the Sylvans. Usually, their businessperson Ed Kuznetsov was my contact, and even he didn't come by that often. Typically, we spoke on the phone when something came up, which hadn't been frequent. Until my life had grown insane with artifacts and belligerent family members, I'd run the place smoothly, taking care of almost every detail about the complex and operations.

"It wouldn't be to talk about that article specifically," Bolin added, "but about the increased crime and the deaths. Nobody's come forward to press charges or anything, but they're worried because people died violently on one of their properties."

"Yeah." I hoped I wasn't about to lose my job. Even if the pay wasn't great, I'd grown comfortable here, and I liked the work and independence. As I'd just been thinking, the owners mostly left me alone, trusting me to handle things. The idea of starting over somewhere else was daunting, especially if some suspicion ended up getting attached to my name. Whether it had been self-defense or not, I had killed those guys. What if someone figured it out?

I made myself skim through the article. "The author is hypothesizing that someone trained animals or *summoned ghost dogs* to kill on their behalf?" I checked the top of the newspaper to make sure it was indeed the *Seattle Times* and not some unreputable rag. Their articles didn't usually cover ghosts.

"Most of the story talks about the idea of trained animals—*real* animals," Bolin said. "It was some of the residents here who suggested ghost animals. Some claimed to have seen dogs or wolves that moved eerily and were unnaturally powerful."

"Nothing *unnatural* about the wolves," came an indignant mutter from inside the apartment—Duncan listening near the door.

I didn't point out that werewolves were all kinds of *unnatural.* We being werewolves ourselves didn't change that.

"Anyway," Bolin said, "I thought you should know about the paper and that my parents would be in touch."

"Yes. Thank you for telling me."

"I also may owe you an apology."

"I doubt you have anything to apologize for. Especially on a Saturday. I wasn't even expecting to see you today."

"I wasn't expecting you to see me either. But, uhm, on my way in..." Bolin looked toward the corner of the building. My apartment was in the back, so we couldn't see the parking lot, but he waved in that direction. "Do you remember how you walked me through onboarding new tenants? And we leased an apartment to those two girls who are going to be roommates?"

I didn't think they were exactly *roommates*, but I hadn't commented on that at any point since Bolin thought the redhead was cute. "I do."

"Well..." He crooked his finger and pointed toward the corner of the building. "I need to show you what's been going on in the parking lot."

"Besides birds defiling your Mercedes?"

He scowled at me. "Yes."

He started to lead me away but noticed the robe and paused. "Uhm, should you get dressed first?"

"Let me grab some flip-flops."

He looked scandalized that I might wander the property in a robe, but it was early on a weekend, so I hardly thought the property-manager dress code applied.

Duncan leaned out, his torso still bare, and looked at Bolin, whose expression grew even *more* scandalized.

While slipping my bare feet into my flip-flops, I noticed that most of the bacon and eggs had disappeared while I'd been speaking with Bolin. All that remained was a plate containing a modest portion. A *very* modest portion. Having Duncan over was *definitely* like sharing a home with a teenager.

I swatted him on the chest before stepping out of my apartment. "Find yourself some clothes by the time I get back, and I'll go to the pond with you."

"Really? You're ready to take on an adventure-filled mission?"

I was ready to not be home if the Sylvans came by. Yes, it was cowardly, and I knew I would have to speak with them eventually, but they wouldn't necessarily expect me to be here on the weekend. If I avoided the complex, I might have until Monday to figure out... whatever I could figure out to tell them. I couldn't admit I was a werewolf with werewolf problems, but I didn't want to lie. Being evasive with the police had been bad enough. The Sylvans were the people who'd paid my salary for years. For *decades*.

"Yeah," was all I told Duncan. "And I need to buy some more eggs from the convenience store. A werewolf with a stomach the size of a football stadium devoured all mine."

"You should pick up eggs *and* bacon," he said without commenting on the rest.

"Do you want to make a list for me?"

He shook his head, but then raised a finger. "Maybe some dark chocolate too."

"High-quality chocolate can't be purchased at a convenience store." I started after Bolin but halted before turning the corner and frowned back at Duncan. "Did you invade my chocolate stash?"

Duncan lifted his hands. "Certainly not, my lady. I know you cherish your sweets."

"Only the sweets that I specifically tuck into the cabinet by the sink." And in the leasing office, and in the maintenance shed by the lawn mower, and in the glove compartment of my truck during months where melting wasn't a problem... "The dark-chocolate variety."

"Yes, I see why you enjoy such fare. And I wouldn't presume to sample yours without permission."

"But consuming all my eggs was okay."

"I've not noticed you gently caressing eggs in your pocket the way you do your chocolate bars."

"I *don't* do that." I hoped I didn't.

Duncan smiled and spread his raised arms, turning the gesture into a deep bow.

Shaking my head, I hurried around the corner. Bolin had been kind enough to get up early, at least by his standards, and bring me that warning. If he had something else to warn me about, I shouldn't impolitely dillydally.

When I caught up to him, he stood on the walkway between the leasing office and the parking lot. With his chin gripped in his hand, he watched two women in their twenties boxing up gear and zipping electronic equipment into bags.

"What's going on?" I asked quietly.

One of the women looked over—the redhead Bolin had admired—and waved cheerfully. She didn't look like a person in the middle of committing a crime or enacting nefarious plans.

"You're a little late to witness it," Bolin said, "but it was a stakeout."

"Were they watching for criminals?"

"Ghosts."

"Ghosts? Like ghost dogs?"

"I didn't ask, but they showed me their ghostometer when I drove in. This is why I felt the need to apologize. Since all the newspaper publicity, well, you probably noticed the people who've applied lately have been a little... quirky, I guess you'd say. *Normal* people get scared away from places where violent deaths occur. Quirky people are attracted to such establishments. It's possible I didn't vet these ladies well enough."

"Their credit scores were fine. I saw the application." Had anything been wrong with them, their employment, or their references, I wouldn't have approved it.

"Their *credit* isn't the problem." Bolin lowered his voice. "I think they're the ones who talked to the *Times* reporter."

"Look, Bolin. I'm glad you want to do a good job leasing this place, but you can only legally check for certain things on the applications."

"You think it's discrimination to deny housing to someone based on whether or not they have a ghostometer?"

"I'm positive. Washington isn't a landlord-friendly state. The tenants have all *kinds* of rights."

"Like... the freedom to perform nocturnal ghost hunts in the parking lot?"

"I'm afraid so. I'm surprised you're not supportive of paranormal activities given that you're..."

He stopped me with a finger to his lips.

"A free spirit yourself," I finished.

"I'm worried that my parents will show up and think I'm not doing a good job. Luna, I have to prove myself capable of handling the accounting and paperwork for this place before they'll let me travel around the world and oversee operations for their other properties. Specifically properties in desirable places that you'd actually want to visit."

"On the behalf of the people of Shoreline, I'm slightly offended."

"You know what I mean." He'd been helpful on numerous occasions and was more mature than I would have guessed when he first rolled up in his G-Wagon, but his voice took on a distinctive whine when he added, "I want to work in Saint Lucia. Or Singapore. Or, oh, did I tell you they got a new property in Ireland? It's where my dad's side of the family came from. I'd *love* to work there for a few months. I could visit the Hill of Tara and New Grange in Boyne Valley." He clutched his hand to his chest with longing.

I thumped him on the shoulder. "Things will work out, Bolin. You're a good intern. I'll let your parents know."

He gave me a dubious look, and I wondered if he knew more than he'd let on about *my* future with the Sylvans. Could they already have an inkling that I was the reason for most of the trouble of late? I grimaced.

A startled gasp came from one of the girls, and she pointed toward the Roadtrek parked in the corner of the lot. No, she was pointing toward the half-naked man trotting barefoot toward it. I sighed. At least Duncan still had my blanket wrapped around his waist.

"It's probably not the ghost hunting that's going to alarm your parents if they show up," I told Bolin.

He groaned and leaned against a tree.

4

"ARE YOU CERTAIN YOU DON'T WANT TO RETURN TO YOUR ABODE AND retrieve the sword?" Duncan asked.

We were at a red light, and he was, fortunately, fully clothed now. He'd replaced his usual black leather jacket with an expensive-looking sweater, a testament to the damp chill of a Seattle winter. With his hand on the steering wheel, he watched as I slid two dollars for gas onto the stack of bills on his dashboard, the fisherman bobblehead still holding them down.

"You think I'll need it to feed ducks?" I asked.

"For adventure and fulfillment."

"At the duck pond."

"Just last night, your cousins appeared to watch you. In your wolf form, especially with the assistance of a fine and devoted male of some stature, you could have defeated them, but what if they'd come when you were a human? You don't carry a firearm loaded with silver bullets, so you may have struggled to deal with them."

"I appreciate the sword, Duncan." I smiled at him to let him know I really did. Further, I hoped he wasn't disappointed that I wasn't toting it all over town on my various errands. "But I don't think it's legal to carry one around openly. They're dangerous weapons. Besides, I don't know anything about sword fighting."

"It is an art with instructors that exist, even in this technology-subsumed era. Perhaps some lessons would be in order. I've noticed local karate dojos with katanas mounted on the walls. A single-edge blade would be different from the dual blade of the longsword, but any experience with swords should be helpful for you."

"I'll think about it, okay?" Given how crazy my life had been lately, I could barely keep up with my work. Taking on a new hobby sounded stressful. He wasn't wrong, however, about my inability to defend myself in human form.

"Certainly."

We turned left at the convenience store and entered a designated wetlands area with the pond sprawling on either side of the road. Duncan turned into a small parking lot near the boardwalk. After stopping, he bounced into the back of his van to collect whatever gear we would need for this endeavor. When I met him outside, he hefted one of his huge cylindrical magnets and the coil of rope attached to it.

"We'll start with this. Maybe we can find enough valuables to trade for eggs and bacon." Duncan tilted his chin toward the convenience store.

Someone was ambling out with a paper bag that probably held a bottle of alcohol. The shopper slumped against a bus-stop sign, looking like he wouldn't wait to get home to start drinking.

There was duct tape covering a crack on a front window of the store that hadn't been there the last time I'd visited. The signs that the neighborhood was growing seedier distressed me.

"I suspect the store owner prefers currency to rusty bike locks and cutlery," I said.

"Americans are fussy, aren't they?"

"We pride ourselves on it."

Duncan led the way along the boardwalk toward the dock jutting out into the water. Ducks paddled toward us.

"They're either starving or not as able to detect our magical and predatory natures as the cats on the premises of your complex," Duncan observed.

"I don't think ducks are as smart as cats." I didn't point out that it was possible that they couldn't sense our magic. It wasn't as if most people could. Though animals—including birds—did tend to be more perceptive.

"Approaching werewolves isn't wise. Though we prefer stimulating prey to hunt, their plumpness could make them targets on a cold hungry night."

"I thought you filled up on bacon and eggs."

"Oh, *I* did. I was thinking of your lurking cousins."

"I'm sure they came all the way to Shoreline to hunt ducks at the pond, yes."

Duncan gave me a wry look, then, before we reached the dock, tossed his magnet into the water. None of the ducks were close enough to be in danger, but they didn't like the noisy splash and squawked and paddled away at top speed. Several took to the air.

"*Now* they'll think twice about approaching werewolves." Duncan nodded, as if he'd done them a great favor.

"'When someone shows you who they are, believe them the first time.'"

He cocked an eyebrow. "Maya Angelou?"

"I think so."

Using the rope, he started pulling the magnet along the bottom of the pond. "She also said, 'Love is like a virus; it can happen to anybody at any time.'"

He only glanced my way instead of giving me a long look laden with significance. That was a relief. We hadn't even slept together yet. I wasn't ready to contemplate deep feelings for my transient treasure-hunting werewolf.

"Did you read a lot of poetry when you were growing up in that lab?"

Though Duncan had shared his past with me, we hadn't discussed how he felt about the reappearance of the man he'd believed long dead or what he thought it meant. That was something I was curious about and more interested in discussing with him than love. I particularly wondered if Abrams and Radomir would continue to be a threat. They were collecting wolf artifacts, and I'd taken back two of the most powerful ones that they'd acquired.

"I read everything I could get my hands on, which was a substantial amount, since Lord Abrams had a library of impressive breadth. That was the part of his castle I most regretted causing to burn. I couldn't regret escaping, but I wished I could have managed it without damaging the home. I even stuck around longer than I should have to try to keep the fire from destroying the library. In hindsight, that's probably what kept me from noticing that Abrams also escaped." Duncan looked at me with an apologetic expression. "There *was* a charred body. All these decades, I believed it had been his, but it might have been the remains of a servant."

"What do you think brought Abrams to Seattle?" I waved north, silently acknowledging that the lavender farm and potion factory outside of Arlington weren't exactly *Seattle*. "Would he have been following you?"

"I don't think so. In thirty years, he hasn't reappeared in my life, even though I wouldn't have been hard to track down, especially since I've started doing that YouTube channel."

"You think that's made you famous, huh?" I couldn't imagine the seventy-five- or eighty-year-old Lord Abrams surfing social media sites for videos on magnet fishing.

"In certain circles, certainly." Duncan lifted his chin as he reeled in his magnet. "A producer for a small television studio in Slovenia once approached me about hosting a show."

"All good films are known to come out of Slovenia."

Duncan squinted at me. "Are you *mocking* me, my lady?"

"I would never." I pointed at the magnet. It was even grimier than other times I'd seen him withdraw it, and I suspected my guess about what *really* covered the bottom of the pond was correct. "That's gross."

Duncan pulled a set of car keys, attached by the metal ring, off the grimy cylinder. He laid them on the railing. "In case someone comes looking for them."

That would be doubtful. They'd probably been down there for years.

Duncan reached for a larger attached item, what looked like a pocketknife, though the gunk coating it made it hard to tell. Before pulling it off, he paused, an odd expression crossing his face. He looked toward the cloudy sky.

"Everything okay?" I asked when he held the pose for several seconds without stirring. "Besides that you should be wearing gloves to touch that magnet?"

"Yes, but..."

Something plucked at my senses, the barest whisper of magic. I looked around for threats, but little had changed. A motorcycle roared on the street passing the convenience store, and someone honked in the distance, but the pond was quiet. Several ducks had settled back into the water at the far end, plucking at bugs floating on the surface.

"It's as if he knows we were talking about them," Duncan muttered so quietly I wasn't sure I'd heard correctly.

"What?"

He shook his head, plucked off the pocketknife, then tossed the magnet back into the water. "Nothing."

I raised frank eyebrows.

He looked over at me with consideration. "I suppose since I seek to earn your trust I can't withhold truths from you."

"That's right." I smiled encouragingly, then held up a finger and delved into a pocket. I withdrew a bar of chocolate, broke off a piece, and held it up so he could see it.

"Are you offering that to solicit the behavior you want from me?"

"It's a bribe to encourage truth-telling, yes."

Duncan wiped his hand off and accepted it. "Soon, I'll be trained so well that the mere rustling of a chocolate wrapper will make me salivate like one of Pavlov's dogs."

"I'll make sure to restock my supply so I've suitable rewards for good behavior."

Duncan slid the chocolate into his mouth and gazed thought-fully toward the cloudy sky again. "For a minute, I felt some-thing... Something magical."

"I got a hint of that too."

"Did you? Hm. Was it calling to you? Almost like the moon's magic? Beckoning you to come?"

"No, I just sensed that magic was in the area."

"I think... the *magic* was summoned elsewhere but beamed in this direction." Duncan waved at the dock, but then, after hesitat-ing, rested his hand on his chest.

"At you?"

"If you didn't feel the call..." He raised his eyebrows, almost hopeful.

I shook my head.

He slumped against the railing, letting his rope droop in his hand, and touched the scar on his forehead. "It felt like the power of the device Abrams has."

I stirred uneasily, barely able to keep from taking a step back from him. "The device that turned you against me?"

He'd been scary as the bipedfuris, especially when he'd sprung at me. I rubbed my shoulder at the memory of him knocking me flying. Even though I'd been in my wolf form, and sturdier than I was as a human, I'd hit the pavers in that courtyard hard. Multiple times.

Duncan noticed my gesture and winced.

"I'm sorry," he said softly.

"It's not going to... I mean, he can't make you attack me from afar, can he?"

"I don't think so. It feels more like he—or whoever is holding the device—is trying to call me back to the north. Back to their home base."

I frowned. "Wouldn't it be Abrams holding the device? He's the one who tuned it to you or whatever, right?"

"It's more than that. He used it in my youth. It's linked to this." Duncan touched his scar again.

I'd once thought it looked like it might have come from a burning cigarette pressed to his skin, but it probably hadn't been something so mundane...

"I'm not sure how that device works exactly, but it's hard for me to resist its power. Its control over me." His voice lowered. "In my youth, Abrams used it to compel me to change into the biped-furis and spread the bite... wanting me to make an army of werewolves for him to command. Luckily for the world, werewolves aren't easily controlled. The ones who changed didn't want to come to him and obey, and I... sometimes I could fight his commands."

Even though he'd alluded to this when he'd told me his story, the admission that he'd actually turned people into werewolves, presumably against their will, disturbed me. My mother lamented the weakening of our kind and the loss of that magic, but I suspected most of the rest of the world would prefer it if were-

wolves permanently lost the ability to infect humans with lycan-
thropy, if we ceased to exist altogether.

"It may or may not be Abrams using the device," Duncan
continued, looking toward the surface of the pond instead of at
me. Lost in memory? "He has a replacement, so he doesn't need
me. I heard them talking about that when they thought me unconscious. Since I betrayed Abrams before—that was *his* word for it—
he doesn't trust that I wouldn't do so again. *He* thought they
should kill me to ensure I wasn't a threat to their plans. Unfortunately, they didn't discuss exactly what those plans were while I
could hear."

I picked at slivers of wood on the railing. "What replacement? I
can see not trusting someone who burned your library down—"

He gave me such an aggrieved look that I believed that had
distressed him more than anything else about the situation.

"—but you're pretty valuable," I finished. "Even irreplaceable.
Unlike eggs and bacon. Which, I'll mention, you haven't wandered
up to purchase yet." Normally, I would buy my own breakfast
foods, but he *had* devoured most of that pound of bacon and eight
or ten of the eggs. What a metabolism.

"I fully intend to make you whole." He bowed to me, then
tossed the magnet into the pond again. "I was hoping we might
find something that could pay for those goods, but I do have cash,
should that prove necessary."

"Even if you find a throne made from gold, I'm pretty sure
you'd still need dollars to buy eggs."

"Such a strange country."

Noticing he hadn't answered my question, I asked, "What
replacement does your Lord Abrams have?"

Duncan was good at avoiding answering questions. Though,
this time, I'd been the one to divert him. Not that a bacon-and-
eggs discussion would have distracted him if he'd truly been dying
to answer.

"The boy."

I blinked, remembering the eight-year-old with floppy brown hair, a young werewolf who'd slipped away during the battle. What he'd been doing there in the first place, I'd never known. He'd *almost* gotten away with my mother's medallion, but I'd traded chocolate to him to get it back. My stashes occasionally did more than satisfy my own addiction.

"You think he kidnapped the boy from a pack and is raising him to do his bidding? Or to... Well, if he's from a modern pack, he wouldn't be able to turn people into werewolves with his bite, right?"

Duncan was walking slowly, pulling his magnet along the other side of the dock, and he gazed at me, his eyes heavy with significance.

"*Did* Abrams kidnap him?" I thought of Duncan's background. "Or do you mean... Abrams isn't carrying around frozen bits of the dead werewolf from the glacier, is he?" It occurred to me that the *dead werewolf from the glacier* had essentially been Duncan. Not a father or a brother or a relative but *him*. They would have been raised differently—*much* differently—so their personalities and experiences would have made them different people, but... what an odd thing to imagine. Like an identical twin, I supposed.

"He didn't discuss it with me—I didn't get much more from that evening than you did—but the boy looks much like I did at that age. I suspect Abrams *has,* for all these years, kept the genetic material from the preserved werewolf. Likely by magical means rather than freezing, but... it would amount to the same."

"So, you're saying that boy was... is..."

Duncan paused in pulling the magnet to rest a hand on his chest. "Exactly the same as me."

5

"THE TERM WOULD BE CLONE." DUNCAN RESUMED PULLING HIS magnet along. "He's my clone. And we're both clones of the original werewolf who lived centuries ago before dying in the mountains and being covered by that glacier."

"This sounds very science-fictional. If you have to do battle with the kid, it becomes a *Star Wars* movie, doesn't it?"

"Only if we use light sabers." Duncan smiled faintly, though there was a troubled crease to his brow.

"Because you're related—uhm, clones—does that make you... responsible for the boy? Or is it all Abrams since he..." I almost said *created*, but that truly did seem sci-fi-ish, prompting me to think of laboratories and test tubes. "Since he was responsible for bringing you—and the kid—into the world."

"I haven't researched the laws on the subject—I had no idea about the boy until we arrived there—but I suppose I could. Since this can now be done with science, no magic required, there probably are some official documents to follow. I would assume, however, that Abrams would be *legally* responsible." A distasteful expression crossed Duncan's face.

Yeah, I wasn't enthused by the idea of Abrams as a legal guardian either, not when his goal had apparently been to form a werewolf army. That might *still* be his goal. Though, if so, I wondered why he'd waited thirty years after Duncan's escape to try again. Twenty-two years, I corrected, assuming my guess at the boy's age was accurate.

"I don't think I would have any legal responsibility," Duncan added after a thoughtful pause, "but I can't help but feel... Now that I know he exists and that he's just a kid..."

"You want to help him," I guessed.

"My childhood wasn't always entirely loathsome—I have fond memories of the times I escaped into the library to read—but it wasn't... pleasant."

That had to be an understatement. I eyed his wrists, though his jacket covered the shackle scars.

"I've been considering if it would be possible for me to return and rescue the boy," Duncan admitted. "He didn't seem like he was being treated that badly, and if he was out hunting in the fields that night, he has more freedom than I ever did, but... I can't imagine Abrams having evolved into a decent father. Even if he *had,* he brought the boy into the world to use him."

"I'm sure he's *not* a decent father. Both those guys were nothing but pushy and manipulative schemers. They tried to have *you* shot, remember. And me kidnapped. And they shot my *mom.* And Emilio. They're bastards. Both of them."

"It's possible the brutes they hired for those missions took liberties with their orders, but Abrams would not have cared about the deaths of anyone involved. Of that I'm certain. And the other man... I obviously do not know him, but he had the vibe of a scheming megalomaniac."

"No kidding."

Duncan paused. His magnet had caught on something. "Even with my strength, I might find it difficult to get back into that compound and retrieve the boy. They *let* us in last time. Because they wanted something from you." He gazed at me.

I shrugged. Radomir had ordered me to touch the medallion, wanting to see what it would do for me. It had glowed brightly but nothing more, as far as I'd been able to tell. Something told me they'd expected more dramatic results.

"They definitely lured us in," I said in agreement. "Laser beams might shoot out if you showed up on the premises again."

Duncan tugged at the magnet, but it didn't rise. "That would also be science-fictional."

"I know. My world has turned very *Star Wars* of late. The next bad guys who show up will be in white stormtrooper armor."

"They'd be much less dangerous than werewolves."

"Are you sure? It would be hard to bite through that armor."

Duncan scoffed and waved a hand. "Easier than opening a can of beans."

I cocked an eyebrow. "Have you done that?"

"No. I rarely crave *beans* when in my werewolf form."

"I don't crave them in my human form either."

"I have used a canine to get into a can of tuna fish." Duncan touched one of his pointed teeth.

"You're a beast."

"As many ladies have told me." He had been grim-faced throughout the discussion of the boy—of his *clone*—but he smiled now, even managing a wink and a bow. The humor faded quickly though, and I could tell the previous week's revelations weighed on him. "I've probably got a bicycle frame here," he said.

"That's not going to buy groceries."

"It could be a safe."

"I'm sure those get heaved into duck ponds all the time."

"You never know." Duncan glanced at the time on his phone, then dug into his pocket. "In case we're not able to find suitable treasure before the store runs out of eggs, here. Please replenish your supply." He tugged out a wrinkled hundred-dollar bill.

"I don't know if they'll make change for that there."

"Change?" Duncan looked blankly at me.

I started to explain but stopped. He probably thought I should buy ten pounds' worth of bacon and dozens and dozens of eggs. "Never mind. If you don't want money back, I'll clean them out."

"Excellent. I'll lever this prize out of the murk." Duncan nodded to me, then grabbed the rope with both hands to put more effort into pulling.

I left him to it, not finding this as much of a fun adventure as he did, though I'd come along more to avoid employers visiting the apartment complex. And spending time with Duncan was pleasant, even if I now worried about the possibility of him being magically forced to turn on me. That had been a concern since the night of our battle, but I'd assumed that for it to happen again Lord Abrams and his magical controller would need to be present. But if he could manipulate Duncan from afar...

I looked back as I climbed a path into the parking lot for the convenience store. Duncan had wrangled his prize onto the dock. It was a dented shopping cart missing its wheels and as covered with grime as everything else. I shook my head in bemusement, wondering how much junk he had to pull out of bodies of water before finding a genuine prize.

"We might have different definitions of adventure, my friend," I murmured but smiled as I entered the store.

A step inside, I dropped the smile and halted abruptly. A man in a ski mask stood in front of the counter, pointing a gun at a gray-haired male clerk, who was pulling money out of the cash register. Another masked man stood behind him in the mouth of an aisle. He held a sawed-off shotgun also pointed toward the counter.

My skin pricked with heat, danger trying to call forth the wolf.

Both men looked toward me. Before I could decide if I should run back outside or let the magic take me over, the guy with the handgun swung it toward me.

Swearing, I dove into the nearest aisle. The gun fired, the blast cracking through the glass door where I'd been standing.

Magic and adrenaline surged through my veins as the change swept over me. There was no tamping it down. All I had the presence of mind to do was tug off my jacket, my keys and phone in the pocket, before my body morphed and fur sprouted from my skin.

Once I stood on all fours in my wolf form, thoughts of *fleeing* from the gunmen evaporated. I was a powerful predator, and these fools had dared challenge me.

When one of the men lunged into view at the end of the aisle, prepared to fire again, I sprang at him. He shouted in surprise but managed to get off a round. I was already charging at him, however, and he flinched back, the bullet going wide. Jaws snapping, I tore into his shoulder. He screamed, dropped the gun, and wheeled away, smashing into a stand and knocking snack bags everywhere.

Engines roared in the parking lot outside—human vehicles. The noise startled me, but movement to my left alerted me to another threat inside. The man with the sawed-off shotgun stepped toward me. Seeing a wolf must have startled him as much as the first man, but he recovered quickly enough to take aim, his hands steady.

An instant before he pulled the trigger, I sprang over shelves, claws clipping bags of chips on the top before I landed two aisles over. Meanwhile, the bullet blew a giant hole in the window beside the door, obliterating the already-taped glass.

I charged out of the aisle as the shooter spun back toward me, but he wasn't fast enough. Before he could swing the gun around to fire again, I sank my fangs into his arm. He screamed, releasing the gun, and stumbled away as he tried to pull free of my grip.

My savage animal instincts wanted me to spring up and tear

out his throat, to utterly destroy this enemy, but I managed to keep my calm. They'd threatened me but not others of my pack, and this wasn't my territory. I wasn't as enraged as some times when I changed, and I kept a measure of sanity.

That didn't keep me from releasing his arm to bite him in the balls. The bastard deserved it.

The next scream was so high-pitched that it hurt my ears. More sounds of engines vrooming came from the parking lot, and I released the man, anticipating a further threat. Nothing good happened to wolves when humans roared close in their noisy metal boxes.

Outside, not cars but motorcycles had entered the parking lot, but they were in an unexpected position—flat on their sides on the pavement. As the two men I'd bitten fled out of the store, both gripping their wounds, I spotted the reason the motorcycles—and their riders—had been knocked down.

Duncan stood among them, fists raised. He remained in his human form, but he was formidable even with his bare hands.

By the time I nosed open the broken door, stepping around shattered glass on the ground, the two riders and the two gunmen, none now armed, were fleeing into the wetlands.

Duncan squinted after them. "If they touch my magnet, I'll kick their asses again."

My wolf brain understood the human words but didn't grasp their full meaning.

Duncan looked at me. "They can have the shopping buggy if they're hard up."

Crunches came from the store—the male clerk stepping gingerly out from behind the counter, over my discarded jacket, and peering toward us. Specifically, his gaze fell upon me. A woman of similar age had come out of a door behind the counter, and she joined him in peering at me.

They weren't threatening, but my hackles rose with the

certainty that danger might result from their scrutiny. Humans did not like wolves.

Duncan patted me on the back. "Why don't you follow those guys and make sure they aren't further trouble, Fluffy?"

Fluffy?

He waved me toward the wetlands and added softly, "I'll get your jacket."

Given that all the men had injuries, delivered by fist or fang, they were unlikely to return, but I sensed the power of the werewolf magic in Duncan, power greater than mine, and allowed that he was like a pack alpha. I trod off, my instincts telling me to stay away from humans anyway, and left Duncan chatting amiably with the store clerks.

Only as I padded into the wetlands did the wolf magic start to fade. I didn't try to track the men, though droplets of blood and the scent of a cigarette one had smoked lingered, so it would have been a simple matter to follow them. Instead, I sat on my haunches by the rolling den that belonged to Duncan and waited for him.

As a wolf, with fur covering my body, nudity wasn't a concern. Only when the magic faded completely, leaving me crouching beside the van, did I come fully back to myself—and realize I was naked in full view of the road.

6

WITHOUT ANY CLOTHES ON, THE DECEMBER AIR WAS COLD. WORSE, a car whizzing past honked before I opened the Roadtrek's door—fortunately, we hadn't locked up—and slipped into the passenger seat.

I was thinking about hunting in the back for something to cover myself with when Duncan opened the driver-side door and hopped in. He dropped his magnet, now detached from the shopping cart, onto the cup holders, then handed me my jacket before turning the key in the ignition.

"We need to skedaddle. Those were the owners of the shop, and they called the police. I tried to convince them you were my dog—sorry about the indignity of that—but they didn't believe it. There was a mirror that looked into that aisle, and the man saw you change." Duncan glanced at me, held up a finger, then ducked into the back, returning with the blanket I'd tied around *his* naked body that morning. "I thought this might come in handy later."

"Thanks." After checking my jacket to make sure my phone and keys were still in the pocket, I draped the blanket over myself. "And thanks for not gawking at my naked body."

"My lady, I would *never* do such a thing."

"Noble."

"A short glance is all I need to sear such memories into my mind to treasure later." Duncan smirked at me before putting the van into reverse.

"I retract my adjective," I stated, though I might have secretly been pleased he *wanted* to remember my nudity and might treasure it. By now, I knew he was attracted to me, but reminders and admissions were pleasing to hear. Even if I wouldn't admit it aloud.

"Maybe I shouldn't have bragged about my memory capabilities." Duncan pointed to the parking lot as we passed the store, the criminals long gone but the two downed motorcycles remaining. "I think those guys were supposed to pick the others up after the robbery. I heard one talking about wanting them to hurry up."

"I wonder if they're related to the motorcycle riders who vandalized our parking lot the day we first met."

Those guys had smashed windows and dented vehicles, not stolen anything, but that was probably only because we'd been there to stop them.

"I don't know," Duncan said. "Are gangs rampant in the area?"

"They didn't *used* to be. This was always a safe suburb within easy commuting distance of Seattle. I never worried about my boys playing outside when they were growing up." I shook my head, lamenting the decline and not wanting to admit it might have gotten worse than I'd realized.

At a red light, Duncan gave me a long look.

"What? You're not going to say I should have brought your sword, are you?"

He snorted softly. "No. You did fine without it. I'll admit I didn't expect you to change in the middle of the store."

"It happened of its own accord when they started shooting at me."

"Understandable. But..."

"The owner got a good look?" I wondered if there'd been a security camera and would be footage. In the face of that, the police might have to reevaluate their belief in werewolves. And if they were able to identify me, they might also connect me to the deaths at the apartment complex.

"Yes," Duncan said. "His wife did too."

I groaned and dropped my head into my lap. Would I have to abandon my job and flee the country? Join Duncan in itinerant treasure-hunting around the world? I didn't long for that. I might want a mission, but I didn't want to travel the world while the law sought me out. I wanted to buy my fourplex and have a comfortable retirement one day. I liked stability, not chaos.

"I don't know if you noticed," Duncan said, "but the wife had a hint of magic in her blood."

"I didn't notice, no. I was busy being indignant about being called Fluffy."

"*That's* what distressed you most?" he asked dryly.

"No. I'm most worried about the possible repercussions of being seen. All I was trying to do was defend myself."

"You also stopped a robbery and possibly saved their lives. You didn't *do* anything wrong."

"I bit a guy in the nuts."

Duncan gaped at me, then dropped a protective—or empathetic—hand over his lap.

"That's assault. A *crime*. Like *killing* people." Was there a frantic note in my voice? Maybe I was *more* than worried about repercussions. "Even if it's all in self-defense, this isn't the Old West. Vigilante justice isn't allowed in Seattle."

"It should be. Whether you meant to be or not, you were a hero." Duncan reached over and rested a hand on my shoulder. "That's why I was giving you that long look."

"Admiration for my ball-biting?" I took a deep breath, willing the panic knotted in my chest to loosen and go away.

"Dear God, no. That's savage. I might possibly be terrified of you now that I know your battle tactics."

"Hilarious."

Releasing my shoulder, Duncan turned the van onto the road leading to the apartment complex. I eyed the parking lot as it came into view, half-expecting to spot police cars waiting for me.

"What I was getting at," Duncan said, "is that you stopped a crime. *Again.* You've protected your apartment complex numerous times now, and you just proved that petty thieves are no match for a werewolf. Now that you're not taking that potion, you could become..." He tilted his palm upward.

"A vigilante?"

"I was thinking superhero. We could arrange that blanket like a cape and make you a mask."

"My dignity doesn't find that any more appealing than being called Fluffy."

"It's a noble mission," he offered. "You did mention you were looking for one. And you've commented more than once that crime has increased in this area."

"Werewolves aren't superheroes. Superheroes don't bite people in the genitals."

"I'm not well-versed enough in comic literature to know if that's true or not."

"Thanks to having raised two sons, I am. It doesn't happen." I let out a soft breath of relief when we pulled into the lot and it was devoid of police cars. At least for the moment.

"Well, no pressure. I'm only offering it up as a potential solution for your spiritual angst."

"My *angst* is fine. Figuring out the secrets of the wolf case is enough of a mission for me right now." I didn't hate the idea of trying to do something about the crime in the area, but... if my

magic turned me into a wolf every time someone held up a convenience store or stole a car stereo, someone would figure out my
identity before long. Unfortunately, the ship might have already
sailed on that.

"I suppose that's also a noble goal." Did Duncan sound a little
wistful?

"You *want* me to become some furry undercover crime
fighter?"

He parked next to my truck. "I'm imagining you in a cape and
mask."

The way he smirked over at me made me ask, "In your imagi-
nation, am I wearing *only* a cape and mask?"

His smirk broadened. "Possibly."

I squinted at him.

He lifted his hands from the wheel. "You can't blame me when
you're modeling your nakedness at this very moment."

I wrapped the blanket around myself and knotted it so I could
dash to my apartment. "A minute ago, you were horrified about
where my wolf bites landed, and now you're fantasizing about my
nudity. Does that strike you as odd?"

"Not at all. I'm male. We can be terrified of and aroused by a
woman at the same time."

"I don't know why I spend time with you."

"You like my flirting and that I call you *my lady*." Duncan
nodded with self-assurance.

I caught myself smiling. He wasn't wrong. What I *really* appreciated was that he kept coming to my assistance. Given all the
trouble finding me lately, I needed that. Hell, I probably needed a
full-time bodyguard. Or ten.

I reached for the door handle, but he lifted his hand and
cleared his throat.

"More seriously, I have an offer. I wasn't sure if I should make it
since... Well, I know you don't trust me fully when it comes to that

case, but I do have the magic detector and some other tools that are helpful with paranormal investigations." Duncan tilted his head toward the back of the van. "I know you've had someone with druidic blood and knowledge studying it, but if you want me to take a look with my equipment, we might be able to learn something more." He shrugged, as if to say he didn't mind either way if I accepted the offer.

I hesitated, debating my answer. Did I trust him around the case now? I believed he was no longer working for my ex-husband, and I was starting to trust him with my life. Daily. That robbery might not have gone as well for me if he hadn't shown up and stopped the motorcyclists. Further, he was the reason I'd found the lavender farm and the stolen artifacts.

"I suppose I shouldn't pass up that offer," I finally said. "The case's mysteries have thus far eluded me."

"Okay. Come on by with it later if you want. I can't promise anything, but my tools are top notch."

"Oh I know. I saw the shopping cart you pulled up." I waved at the magnet.

"A feat that I'm positive impressed you."

"So much so that I'll be fantasizing about you in a blanket and a mask tonight."

"I wouldn't be offended in the least by that."

My phone rang. I withdrew it warily, not sure whether to expect the police, my belligerent cousin, or some new plague on my life. My son Austin's name popped up.

"Oh!"

I held up a finger to Duncan, tightened the blanket around myself, and hopped out of the van to answer.

Since my youngest son had been doing his Air Force training across the country, I hadn't seen him in months, and he'd only called a few times during that time. Because, he'd promised me, his phone use was restricted, not because he didn't love his mother and care about keeping her updated. It had sounded like a partial truth, but I'd reluctantly accepted that my boys didn't need their mom as much anymore. At least Austin had had more time to process his lack of a college fund, and he wasn't, as far as I knew, holding a grudge, not like Cameron.

"Hey, Austin," I answered, striving to sound casual instead of like a parent starved for updates. "How's Mississippi?"

He was doing his training at Keesler Air Force Base there.

"Hi, Mom. It's okay. Not as humid now."

"How's it going?" I wondered what had prompted the rare call. "You haven't fallen out of an airplane or anything, have you?"

"I'm training to be a cyber-operations technician, Mom." His voice was dry, the eye roll assumed.

"They cyber-operate in planes sometimes, don't they?"

"Not yet. I'm fine. We've got leave for Christmas. I told Andrew and Chul I'd see them over the holidays. We might even play a gig."

"That's great. I'll pretend you want to see your mother too, not just jam with your high-school friends."

"Of *course* I want to see you." The tone promised another eye roll. "I need a place to stay."

"I knew your love and faithful devotion would bring you back to me."

"Ugh, don't say things like that. I'm right outside the mess hall. Someone might hear."

I reined in further snark and said a non-embarrassing, "I'm sorry. When can I expect you?"

"My plane comes in on the twentieth. Andrew said he'd pick me up at SeaTac."

"That's good of him. I'll get a few groceries."

"Cool, thanks. See you then." He hung up.

I returned my phone to my pocket, delighted that at least one of the boys would come home for the holidays, but that meant I needed to do a few things. "Get the tree out of storage, visit Costco, and..." I gazed around the parking lot and especially into the woods. "Make sure my damn cousins leave me alone for Christmas and that no *crime* invades my territory."

I scowled, my delight at the prospect of seeing my son tainted by my new fear that the world was on the verge of figuring out I was a werewolf. For the boys' entire lives, I'd taken a potion that sublimated my lupine magic and had striven to be a normal and entirely *human* mother. They had no *idea* about my secret.

A flutter of anxiety taunted my stomach as I worried whether that would change during Austin's visit.

7

I NOT ONLY DRAGGED MY PERSONAL CHRISTMAS TREE OUT OF storage but put up the big outdoor one for the complex. The decorating included draping strings of lights all over it and the lampposts. While I worked near the parking lot, I eyed the entrance every time a car drove in, dreading the arrival of the police. Surely, the store owners had shared the video footage of me—in both incarnations of myself—with the authorities by now.

Instead, Duncan's Roadtrek turned in and presumptuously parked in one of the staff spots next to my truck. Since he stepped out with a box of groceries containing more than cartons of eggs and packages of bacon, I didn't berate him.

"We were interrupted earlier," he said as he walked up with the load, "so I didn't get to acquire your supplies."

"I still have your hundred." I dug into my pocket and held it out, glad it had been in the jacket that I'd removed before changing. One of my favorite pairs of jeans and a super soft hoodie had disappeared into the ether. Fortunately, I'd made a Goodwill trip earlier in the week and had picked up a few things.

Duncan eyed the bill. "I'd tell you to keep it, but I suspect I'd later find it on my dash with your gas money."

"That's right. This was your money to start with." I waved it toward the box. "What's all that? More than bacon and eggs."

"Yup. I heard you're going to have another mouth to feed. And we all know how big *my* mouth is."

"I'm not sure that's a bragging point, buddy."

"Perhaps not."

"You were listening to my phone call?"

"Not intentionally, but my hearing is excellent, and you didn't wander far before answering it. Will you allow me to meet your son or hide me away like an embarrassing foot wart?" Duncan smiled as he asked, but there was an intentness in his brown eyes, as if my answer might matter.

Did he *want* to meet my son? When he'd met the rest of my family—the werewolf side of my family—they'd tried to kill him. All except my niece Jasmine, who thought he had a sexy accent. Admittedly, Mom hadn't attacked him, but she was old and had cancer. I needed to visit her this holiday season too, even if she'd informed me on numerous occasions that werewolves weren't Christian and didn't celebrate Christmas. She hadn't been amused when I, as a rebellious teenager, had draped tinsel over her tail.

"I'm not sure how I'll *explain* you," I said, "but Austin will probably love you. You live in a van full of geeky tech equipment."

"It *is* a posh setup."

"So posh that I had to sit on your gear shift this morning because there was so much crap in the seat well that it overflowed."

"Next time, you can sit in my lap. You know, for your comfort."

"I'd still get pronged by something."

He grinned wickedly as he took the hundred and nodded in the direction of my apartment. "May I put these items in your fridge?"

"Yes, thank you. Oh, and there's a stack of clothing on the table for you."

"Clothing?"

"We've both had a few unexpected changes of late. I used some of my clothing budget to pick up a few things for you."

"That's very thoughtful." Duncan looked a little bemused—maybe women didn't buy him clothing that often—but bowed and said, "Thank you." After taking a couple of steps, he paused. "After you're finished there, do you want to use some of the geeky equipment in my van to examine your case?"

I glanced at the time on my phone. Darkness had fallen, and it was after five. The calls from tenants and prospective tenants had dwindled, and I was technically off for the day.

"Okay."

"I have a special treat waiting for you in there," he called as he carried the groceries up the walkway.

"I'm not sitting in your lap," I called after him.

He grinned back over his shoulder at me. It was a handsome grin, and I couldn't help but return it. I tried to rub the expression off my face and tamp down my feelings. There was too much to do —too many problems to solve—and now, with Austin coming soon, I had a deadline.

I didn't truly know if I would introduce Duncan to him since my sons might see it as a betrayal if I dated someone besides their father. But, after all the help Duncan had given me, I also didn't want to shoo him away and tell him not to park here until after the holidays. Since he was a visitor to the Seattle area, he probably didn't have any other friends or family here that he could celebrate with. Of course, if he followed my mom's beliefs, he would be indifferent to Christmas—unless I draped tinsel over his tail.

My phone rang, a number I didn't recognize, and I answered it warily. "Hello?"

"Hello, is this the werewolf?" a woman with a stern voice asked.

It sounded familiar, but I struggled to place it. It couldn't be the female owner of the convenience store, could it? I hadn't heard her speak.

"Uhm, this is Luna."

"The werewolf," came the confident reply. "Unless you've changed your mind and have imbibed one of my potions?"

Oh, it was the alchemist. Rue.

"I haven't yet but not because there's anything wrong with them. I'm sure they're of high quality."

"Of *course* they are. I only use organic, free-range snake skins and slug slime."

"I do hate factory-farmed slug slime."

"Everyone does. It affects the efficacy of the potions. Do you still have an apartment for rent?"

I blinked at the abrupt topic shift, and it took me a moment to remember I'd mentioned that when Duncan and I had visited her graffiti-laden home downtown.

"I... think we have one vacating soon. I can check the date."

The news stories on the complex had been a mixed blessing. After the parking-lot crimes, we'd lost some tenants, but we'd also gained new ones, those *drawn* by notoriety, such as the ladies who would probably be out setting up their ghost-hunting equipment soon.

"Very good. Do let me know if one is available and of decent size for storing equipment, books, and ingredients."

"The one coming up is a two-bedroom."

"*Perfect*. The tenants in my current complex have grown tedious, and, as I informed you, the landlord blames *me* for the graffiti that ill-educated and bigoted neighbors leave on and around my door. The kindly but pushy grandmother who hands me bibles is no more welcome. I do not live in sin. I help the para-normal community with their problems."

"I believe you. It's common for the paranormal to be misun-derstood by their mundane neighbors."

"Yes, this is a certainty. I crave an outdoor entrance and a facility that allows pets such as dogs. *Large* dogs."

"Up to sixty pounds with some breed restrictions," I murmured the line from our lease paperwork automatically.

Rue hadn't had a dog when we'd visited before, had she? Maybe she wanted them around the premises for protection purposes.

"Are the werewolves not more than sixty pounds?" she asked.

"Yeah, but they're not pets."

"They would, being territorial and quite powerful, effectively protect the residents from crimes, though, yes?"

"They would, but I'm also trying to cut down on the amount of crime."

If she'd heard about all the craziness here, it was surprising she wanted to move up. Though maybe not. She could probably handle herself against criminals; graffiti-leaving grandmothers might be more difficult to deal with since propriety demanded a gentler hand when dealing with one's elderly neighbors.

"Excellent. Do inform me when you learn the date that the unit will be available. My granddaughter has already promised to help me pack. She agrees that this domicile is not wholesome for me."

And ours *was* wholesome?

"Okay," was all I said and hung up.

Duncan had returned, carrying the stack of clothing I'd offered him, and caught the tail end of the call.

"I predict a change in the demographics of your tenants," he said.

"If you mean we're attracting more weirdos these days, I'm afraid you're right."

Duncan touched his chest, eyes innocent.

"Yes, you."

"Huh. A question about these garments, if you don't mind." He held up a sweater. "They don't have tags. I assume it's not because they were handwoven, like my fine cashmere sweater from the Alps."

"No, they're not handwoven."

As if. He'd seen my budgeting envelopes. There wasn't money in any of them for clothes spun by artisans in exotic mountain homes.

Duncan held up the sweater, turning it left and right. "Were any of these items not to fit, where would I take them to exchange them?"

"Goodwill."

"That is a store?"

"Yeah. They sell quality stuff at a bargain because it's been worn before."

"Worn before?" he mouthed, as if the concept were foreign to him.

"Yup. I call it experienced clothing. It's been places and seen things."

His mouth dangled open. For a guy who scrounged rusty bike frames off lake bottoms, he seemed shocked by the idea of thrifting.

"For obvious reasons, werewolves shouldn't have expensive clothing. You won't cry if this stuff disappears. Besides, my kids grew up wearing secondhand stuff, and they're fine. Neither of them is in therapy." I paused, less certain that was true now that they didn't live with me. "Not for that anyway," I amended.

"I see. Yes, quite practical." Duncan lowered the sweater.

"More so than a blanket." I'd finished with the decorations and pointed to his van. "I'll get the case and meet you there. Unless you already snagged it when you were in my apartment?"

Even if I'd decided to trust him around the artifact, the question might have been a test. How much did he want to investigate it further?

"I didn't presume to snag it, no. Especially given its last known storage location."

Yeah, he'd balked at touching my tube of hormone cream. I'd actually moved the case from that dresser drawer back to the heat duct. The fewer people who knew its location the better.

"Good." I patted his shoulder, then strode to my apartment.

Inside, I used my trusty oven mitt to retrieve the case. As usual, the magic tingled unpleasantly against my hand, even with the insulation.

To fortify myself, and tide my empty stomach over until dinner, I grabbed a couple of squares of chocolate. Before leaving, I peeked in the fridge to see what Duncan had left.

"Wow."

There were six cartons of eggs, a stack of packages of bacon, sliced salami, traditional link sausages, five pounds of ground beef, and two ready-bake pizzas laden with pepperoni, sausage, and Canadian bacon. There wasn't a sign of a vegetable, save for a tub of sauerkraut that had been there for weeks, maybe months, hunkering in the back behind my Greek yogurt.

"Austin really is going to love him," I muttered.

My boys weren't werewolves, but they did share the largely carnivorous traits of my kind.

When I returned to the van, the sliding door was open, a light on in the back. The Roadtrek had solar panels that I'd noticed tilted southward on Seattle's rare sunny winter days, but my senses tingled a bit as I approached. The source of illumination was a glowing pendant dangling from the ceiling, not a light fixture.

"Are you ready for me?" I asked, leaning in.

At first I didn't see Duncan, but he was in the front, knees on the passenger seat and butt toward me as he dug into the boxes under the dashboard.

"I'm *always* ready for you, my lady," he said, his voice muffled.

"I should have assumed that."

"Given my healthy stamina and vigor, most assuredly."

I squeezed past the tiny sink and under-counter refrigerator and opened a narrow door, wondering if it revealed a closet. No, I'd found the bathroom, a bathroom *smaller* than a closet. There was a tiny corner sink and a showerhead, but was that a composting toilet? I wondered about the plumbing arrangement. Maybe he only had use of the shower and sink when he was at a campground with water hookups. Or... a parking lot with a hose? Since I'd never had an RV or even been camping in one, the workings were nebulous to me.

I closed the door and moved to the table immediately adjacent to the bathroom. In the van, everything was immediately adjacent to everything else.

The built-in padded bench seats were buried under boxes of gear and rusty treasures, with the area underneath the table equally packed. Cabinets and racks filled the wall space, blocking more than one window, and a bicycle was mounted flat to the ceiling, a pedal dangling low enough that I had to duck. Entering the van felt like climbing into a hoarder's closet. The twin bed was the only place to sit. I perched on the edge of the mattress, stuff piled underneath bumping the backs of my legs, and set the case on the table.

To my lupine vision it had glowed, but to my human eyes it was merely aged ivory, the sides carved with decorative vines, leaves, and flowers, and the wolf head prominent on the lid. The hinges and clasp were small, even delicate, and looked like they wouldn't keep a determined person from getting inside, but its unpleasant tingle grew into a more jolting electric zap if one tried.

"I'm delighted to have you join me in my abode, my lady." Duncan bowed, as much as he could in the tight space, and almost clunked a pair of goggles he was wearing on the door to the bathroom. "I see you brought your sexiest attire." He pointed to the oven mitt.

I removed it and rested it on the table. "I know how much kitchenware turns you on."

"Quite. I hope you approved of the groceries I brought to replace what I ate." He peered through the goggles at the case.

"You more than replaced what you ate."

"As one should do if one hopes to be invited back. With these on, the case glows silver with a blue nimbus." Duncan tapped the goggles, then pushed them onto his forehead and opened an upper cabinet. He withdrew the magic detector I'd seen before, a boxy device with antennae that reminded me of old-fashioned divining rods.

"It sounds similar to the view I had with my wolf eyes." I didn't remember a blue nimbus though.

If that had significance, he didn't explain it. "I can't see through the sides to get a gist as to the contents."

"Are those *X-ray* goggles?"

"Not exactly, but sometimes you can see magical items, at least their blurry outlines, through walls and floors and such. I *almost* wore these when I visited your apartment with my magic detector, but you were already suspicious of me."

"Yeah, guys who wander into my bedroom with X-ray goggles are extra sus."

"Indeed."

"Even as we speak, I'm wondering if I should be wearing a lead apron." I squinted at him and crossed my arms over my chest. My boobs probably weren't magical enough to glow through walls or whatever, but who knew. My blood *was* paranormal.

"I've already seen you naked."

"And imprinted it in your memory. Yes, I remember."

"Since the case itself is magical, I didn't expect to be able to see through the sides, but it was worth checking." After removing the goggles, he turned on the magic detector.

It beeped happily, the antennae drawn toward the case.

Since we'd already determined it was magical, I merely raised my eyebrows. Duncan pushed up a hinged lid on the back of the device, something I hadn't noticed before, and showed me a small window where information was displayed. A header claimed an 87 percent certainty that the case had been made with druidic magic but also gave a 10 percent possibility to shamanic origins. A bullet list included silver, nacre, and Siberian mammoth ivory, as well as a number of metals, including gold, iron, and cobalt.

"*Mammoth* ivory?" I asked, assuming those were items present in the artifact.

"Oh yes. It's quite rare, naturally, but there are preserved specimens available, and people do carve with it."

"I guess we at least know an endangered species wasn't illegally poached to make this."

"I don't imagine poaching was illegal when mammoths roamed the Earth, no. Getting one meant the village wouldn't starve that winter."

"Yeah." I leaned back. The information was interesting but didn't tell me much that I hadn't known. The nacre—that was mother-of-pearl, wasn't it?—probably lined the inside of the case. And the metals... "The hinges are silver, right? Do you think those other metals are mixed with it?"

"I... think this may be a list of the contents that make up the case but may also be giving us a clue about what's inside."

"Metal stuff?"

"Apparently."

Duncan turned off the detector and grabbed a small tin I'd seen before. He dug a finger into its contents—some kind of glowing violet gunk the viscosity of lip balm—and rubbed the stuff over his hands. It would allow him to touch the case without being zapped. A better solution than an oven mitt.

Once he'd coated his hands, he tried unfastening the clasp. As before, it didn't move, and neither did the lid.

"I've seen you rip open a steel door," I said.

"Yes, and I could apply more force here, but..." Duncan turned the case over, eyeing it from all angles as whatever was inside clunked about. "I would prefer not to damage it, both because it's a valuable magical artifact in its own right and because there might be a backlash."

"Backlash like the magic knocking you through the windshield?"

"That's a distinct possibility." Duncan set the case down and delved into one of his storage containers. "I am undeniably curious about the contents though. What's inside that can heal venom, poison, and werewolf bites?"

"What kinds of things are usually made using cobalt?" I had no idea, but a guy who fished for metal and magic for a living ought to know.

"Lots of items have cobalt in them. Batteries, pigments, drying agents, tooth implants..." Duncan poked in the storage container as he spoke. "It's also used in superalloys for gas turbine and aircraft engines."

"Oh yes. An aircraft engine. *That's* what must be in the case."

He lifted out one of his magnets with a flourish. "Cobalt is also used in these."

"Magnets?"

"Yes." Duncan held it over the case without touching it. A thunk sounded as the item inside hit the bottom of the lid.

"That's kind of interesting," I said, though I wasn't sure it clued us in that much about the contents. "Did druids usually make artifacts out of metal?"

"I don't think they made armor and weapons out of metal, but they did use bronze, copper, and lead for some of their artifacts. And possibly cobalt, though I don't know if I've heard of that specifically."

"I can ask Bolin."

After causing the item within to thunk against the lining of the case a few more times, Duncan sighed and put away his magnet.

"Do you think Radomir and Abrams know what's inside?" I asked.

For that matter, had Chad known? When I'd eavesdropped, he'd sounded like he knew more about the case than he'd told Duncan.

"I don't know."

"If they knew *everything* about it and the other artifacts they were collecting, they wouldn't have needed me to come up and touch things."

"They only cared about you touching your mother's medallion, though, right?"

"True. I was the one who was poking everything else to buy time. Still, it seemed like they might be in the studying process. Maybe they're collecting everything they can related to were-wolves, because..." I shrugged and looked at Duncan. He was more likely to know at least Abrams' motivations than I.

"It could be a key." Duncan made a turning motion in the air.

"A magical key?"

"Sure. To open a magical vault somewhere, perhaps. A *big* one buried in a mountain and guarded by a dragon. It could be full of ancient and exotic treasures." His eyes gleamed at the notion.

"I would accuse you of avarice, but you consider rusty bike locks to be treasures. I think you just like the search."

"I do enjoy the challenge, and I'm willing to sift through lesser items, sometimes referred to as junk, to find more interesting prizes."

"Since you gave me a sword you presumably found, I won't suggest that your efforts are futile."

"Certainly not. How do you think I afford my opulent life-style?" Duncan spread his arms, his knuckles bumping both sides of the van.

"You have a composting toilet."

"An opulent one."

"Oh, is it gilded?"

"No, but it's self-incinerating." He waggled his eyebrows, as if that might get me excited.

"So it's as likely to hurl you through the windshield as the artifact."

"Not quite. For your edification, not because I feel the need to prove the value of my chosen career to you, I *have* found vaults before. Safes, at least. There was one that I swam down to pull out of a barnacle-covered sunken ship on the bottom of the ocean. In the dark and dangerous depths, I had to twist and turn through tight passageways, almost getting stuck more than once."

"Was the ship guarded by a dragon?"

"A killer whale, actually."

"Did it kick your ass?"

"No. Despite the name, killer whales are pretty mellow. This one showed off by swimming around with a dead salmon on its head like a hat. Apparently, that's an orca trend that comes in and out of fashion."

"I know a dead fish is something I'd enjoy wearing."

"No sillier than high-heeled shoes, I'd think."

I couldn't argue with that.

"Anyway, when I pulled up the safe and drilled into it, it contained a pile of gold and silver coins from the 1600s. It was quite the lucrative adventure and funded all my expenses for some time. I was so chuffed that I used some of the proceeds to buy buckets of salmon for the whale. It ate them instead of wearing them, though."

"You're an interesting werewolf."

"A fascinating one, I should think."

Movement outside one of the windows drew my eye. A car I didn't recognize rolled into one of the guest spots. I groaned because I *did* recognize the driver and his passenger. The owners of the convenience store.

I peered behind their car, anticipating a number of police vehicles trailing them into the parking lot. I didn't see them, but the way the couple gazed intently through the windows at me promised they hadn't come to ask about apartment vacancies.

8

"I SENSE YOUR COUSINS AGAIN," DUNCAN SAID.

I halted, my hand on the sliding door to his van. I'd been about
to hop out to see if the convenience-store owners had come to
extort, threaten, accuse, or—the least likely option—thank me.
"What? Where?"

Duncan nodded toward the greenbelt. "You may want to hide
the case somewhere more secure than your sock drawer."

It had been in the heat duct under the bed, but if Augustus
broke into my apartment with something like Duncan's magic
detector, he would be able to find it. It was also possible he would
be able to sense its power through the floor.

"I *may* want to kick their asses," I said, irritated that they were
lurking around again.

"Let me know if I can help. There are three or four of them
close enough for me to detect."

I couldn't sense any of them but trusted that Duncan could
pick out magical beings from farther away. After all, he was an
ancient glacier werewolf. The clone of someone who'd been born

into a far more magical time, his ancestors closer to the first of our kind that had been created.

"Let me see what these guys want first." I nodded toward the recently arrived car. The woman remained in the passenger seat, but the man had stepped out and seemed to be waiting for me. "I'd prefer *not* to change into a werewolf in front of them again. On the off-chance that they were too busy being scared for their lives to notice exactly what happened in their aisles."

Duncan had already said they'd seen me in the store's mirror, but he nodded. "Okay. While you talk to them, I might saunter over to that path to glare menacingly into the woods."

"Put some more dog-poop bags in the holder while you're there, will you? I noticed it was almost empty again."

He gaped at me. "How am I supposed to menace your foes while holding bags for the gathering of canine *excrement*?"

"You can't be bothered by such things. Not when you were just bragging about the opulence of your toilet to me. The bags are in the maintenance shed, shelf to the left of the door." I thumped him on the arm before hopping out. "Thanks for being such a useful visitor."

"Is there any chance my ongoing support is going to get me an invitation to your bedroom?"

"There's a chance."

I started to smile, but the store owner stepped into view. I took a deep breath, bracing myself for whatever he had come to talk about. That the couple had known where to find me was distressing but probably not surprising since his wife had the blood of a paranormal being. A witch? Maybe a clairvoyant. They were good at finding people, especially others with paranormal tendencies.

"We don't have any vacancies right now," I told the man, "but I'm starting a waiting list if you want to be on it."

He blinked a few times, looked at his wife, and then back to me. Then *he* took a bracing breath and met my gaze. Maybe he wasn't here to extort me.

"I have come to thank you for perhaps saving my life and without a doubt the contents of my cash register," he said, surprising me, "and also to ask you for a favor."

"Uhm. You're welcome."

He looked at his wife again. She nodded firmly at him, though she remained in the car. Why did I imagine her prodding him in the back with a stick to direct him toward a lion's cage? Or... a wolf's den?

"I am Minato. That is my wife, Mayumi. We have two daughters that are in college, and everything we earn from our store, we give to them for the great expense of having a fine education in this country. We take very little for ourselves, only enough to live modestly in our home, which we can only afford because we purchased it more than thirty years ago, when we first came to America." He held up a phone with a cracked screen and a photo of a family of four posing in front of a tidily maintained 1950s rambler of about a thousand square feet. They proliferated in the area.

I nodded, though I didn't know where this was going. He couldn't think I was wealthy and could give him money, could he?

"We are currently paying... *taxes*—" his face twisted with distaste, "—to the Snohomish Savagers."

"Oh." My shoulders slumped as I remembered Francisco, the bartender and owner of El Gato Mágico, also complaining about having to pay money to my pack. He'd been apprehensive about me when I'd walked in, believing the family had sent me to collect an extra payment.

"Are you a lone wolf? Do you perhaps fight the injustice of that pack?" Minato raised his gray eyebrows hopefully.

"I, ah. I'm actually... Well, I know that pack well. And I think I know the guy who's been coming to demand taxes from you."

"Augustus," his wife said, leaning out the window. "A noble name for such an *ignoble* brute."

"I agree." I glanced over my shoulder, noticing Duncan walking across the lawn.

Was he heading toward the maintenance shed to get the bags? Damn, I was starting to like him for more than his willingness to protect me.

"We cannot afford what he demands of us," Minato continued. "And these payments have not thus far come with the protection he promised. He said the pack would improve the neighborhood and drive off the gangs and criminals that have moved into the area, but he only shows up when he wants money. From what we have seen, he does *nothing*, and the only violence that is averted is that which he threatens us with if we do not pay promptly."

"Augustus doesn't even live around here," I said before realizing I had no idea where he currently made his home. This was barely Savager territory though. As the name suggested, the pack mostly considered Snohomish County theirs, and the convenience store was a few miles into King County. El Gato Mágico, in the heart of Seattle, was *more* than a few miles into it. "Is he only extorting people with, ah, paranormal tendencies?" I looked at the wife—Mayumi—wondering if she would admit to having magical blood. A lot of people didn't. Some didn't even know they had it, other than being aware that they, for some reason, had psychic gifts.

"That is what we have heard." Minato nodded. "Maybe, because we sense their kind and understand their power, we are more... susceptible to their threats." He grimaced. "It is possible they extort others as well."

"They're huge *bullies*," Mayumi said out the window.

"I know. What do you want me to do?" I didn't blame them for seeking a solution to their problem, but I didn't know how to get Augustus to stop being a bully. If I did, he wouldn't be lurking in the greenbelt, poised to steal the artifact as soon as I left it unguarded. "For what it's worth, I don't think the whole pack is behind the extortion. Augustus and some of his siblings are taking it upon themselves to be..."

"*Penises*," Mayumi said when I didn't find an appropriate word quickly enough.

Minato said something stern to her in their native language. Not cowed, she answered equally sternly and gesticulated for emphasis.

Minato faced me again. "They are using their supernatural strength to threaten and take advantage of us. Months ago, we tried to call the police, but they did not believe us when we mentioned these miscreants were werewolves. The law enforcers in this area are *very* ignorant about paranormal threats."

I grunted noncommittally, glad the police didn't believe in werewolves. Thus far, that had helped me avoid being implicated in anything.

"Did you call the police today?" I asked.

"Only to make a report for our insurance provider. We did not mention anything paranormal." He looked frankly at me. "Or lupine."

"That's good."

"As we've observed, the police are unhelpful to us overall. Even when they make arrests, the justice system here often allows criminals to walk free." Minato shook his head. "This was not the way when we first moved to this country. This recent trend is woeful."

"Yes." I kept my face neutral and didn't show my relief at learning they hadn't told the authorities about me. That meant there wasn't a police sergeant somewhere perusing video footage of me changing into a wolf in the potato-chip aisle.

"You are local and understand our problems." Minato waved toward the parking lot, and I was positive he'd seen the various news stories of late.

"That is true."

"Today you proved you are a good neighbor and have the power to protect people. You not only have the power but you *use* it."

Since my last potion had worn off, that was true, but my magic taking over had been the reason for my intervention at their store, not a conscious decision.

"We would like to pay *you* to protect us," Minato said as his wife nodded firmly.

"I'm afraid I already have a job."

Duncan leaned out of the maintenance shed, holding boxes of doggie bags. "Do you want the green ones or the black ones that turn into little mitts?"

"A glamorous and fulfilling job," I told Minato as I pointed to the black bags and made a shooing motion toward the path and the dog clean-up station.

"We understand you are busy, but your services are greatly needed by the community. Should you agree, we know other businessowners like us, and we might be able to scrape together extra money to make patrolling the neighborhood worth your time." Minato hesitated. "We would, of course, need you to defend us from the Savagers. In order to amass funds for you, we would need to stop paying Augustus."

"Look, you don't have to pay me, okay? I'll try to figure out something to help you. I'll talk to the pack leader."

"If you protect us from Augustus and his cronies, we will insist on paying you."

"That's not necessary. You shouldn't have to *pay* anyone for protection. Most werewolves just want to be left alone to lead their lives and hunt during the full moon. They're not supposed to be like the mafia."

"Anything you could do would be greatly appreciated." Minato nodded to me before returning to the car.

As they drove away, Duncan joined me. "Your cousins disappeared from my senses as soon as I finished with the bags and glared menacingly into the woods."

"*You're* the person the local business owners should be hiring for protection."

"I don't have a superhero cape."

"My blanket is still in your van." I looked toward the woods, having a feeling that Duncan's presence was the only reason my cousins hadn't attacked. I also worried about leaving the premises. As often as they were coming by, they had to be biding their time and waiting for a chance to sneak into my apartment and look for the case. I would have to take it with me every time I went somewhere.

"Are you going to try to stop your cousins from extorting the populace?" Duncan must have caught some of the conversation.

"I'll talk to Lorenzo. I've been meaning to go up to see Mom anyway."

"Didn't you say he forbade your cousins from pestering you?"

"Yeah."

"They don't seem to be listening."

"I've noticed. I was away from the pack for so long that I don't know how many alphas have come and gone over the years, but it sounds like Lorenzo is mostly in the position because he's my mother's mate, and she's always been a strong female leader for our people. It also sounds like my cousins have challenged Lorenzo, or they've at least been posturing, and don't fully respect him."

"It sounds to me like they need to be driven out of the pack."

"I don't think there's anyone strong enough to do that." Alone, I was a match for Augustus, but he had a lot of allies.

"I would be *happy* to drive them out." Duncan's eyelids drooped halfway, a feral vibe emanating from him. When he wasn't smiling and being deliberately goofy, he was a little scary.

"You're not a part of the Savagers. They won't listen to you." Despite my words, the thought of unleashing Duncan on my cousins made me wistful, but I doubted the family politics would allow that as a solution. Duncan had *already* thumped my cousins, and that hadn't improved their behavior.

"I wasn't going to drive them out by *talking* to them," he said.

"You've already kicked their asses, and they're still here."

"They're not fast learners, are they?"

"Well, they've figured out not to attack when you're by my side."

"That's something at least." Duncan lifted a hand to my shoulder, as if to say he would be pleased to remain by my side.

I didn't want to need a man, to need *anyone*, but I caught myself leaning into his touch, glad for his presence.

"Do you want to come with me to visit my mom?" I asked.

"Yes," he said promptly.

"Even though you'll probably be attacked?"

"Yes."

"Why?" I asked softly, looking into his eyes.

"I don't know if you've noticed this, but I'm kind of into you."

"Because you looked at my chest with the X-ray goggles on?"

He grinned. "I don't need goggles to notice your fine attributes, but I also like the way you snark at me, and I'm having all *kinds* of adventures simply because I'm in your orbit."

"My adventures didn't start until the day you showed up. It's possible your presence *causes* them to occur." Admittedly, I couldn't blame him for more than finding the wolf case, though that *was* at the core of a lot of the chaos. Even if he'd somehow been responsible for everything, I couldn't wish he had never ambled into my life.

"I do strive to make the world an interesting place. I..." Duncan looked off to the north, a troubled expression replacing his grin.

"Is that device calling to you again?"

"Yes, but I can resist it." Duncan nodded firmly and pointed to his van. "I'll drive you up to see your mom. I'm eager for another wolf to jump on my hood and leave claw marks on it."

"We could take my truck. Additional scratches in the paint wouldn't be noticeable."

"Would I then have to leave gas money on your dashboard?"

"Obviously. That's how it works." I smiled but waved away the idea—he'd bought me far more groceries than he'd eaten, so I couldn't charge him for anything.

Before we'd taken more than a few steps toward the truck, Bolin's SUV rolled into the parking lot.

I didn't think much of it until I spotted additional people inside. His earlier warning that his parents might come by came to mind, and I groaned. If only Duncan and I had cleared out five minutes earlier. We would have been gone when they'd arrived.

9

"THESE ARE MY EMPLOYERS," I SAID AS BOLIN'S SUV PARKED, HIS parents gazing out the windows in my direction. "Try to keep your clothes on and be... normal."

Duncan's eyebrows arched. "*Normal?*"

Yeah, that would be a stretch for him even if he tried.

"Maybe you could wait in your van." I waved toward the Roadtrek.

It would be easier if I didn't have to explain his eccentricities. Or his feral vibe.

What if Bolin's dad had enough magic in his blood to sense what Duncan was? When I'd had meetings with my employers in the past, I hadn't noticed Rory Sylvan had a paranormal aura, but unless the druidic talent skipped a generation, he had to have some power. It had probably been because my senses had been dulled by the potion that I'd missed it before. Now, as they climbed out of the big SUV with their businessperson Ed Kuznetsov, who was my usual contact, I wiped my palms on my jeans, nervous. Rory Sylvan might have known all along that I wasn't any more normal than Duncan.

"I'll wait in your truck," Duncan said. "We have a date, remember?"

"Going to see my mom counts as a date?"

"Maybe she'll make us dinner. Is she domestically inclined?"

I almost laughed, but I recalled that he'd only seen her from a distance, so he didn't know. "She's a strong, independent, and fierce werewolf. She might drop a raw elk haunch on the ground for you to gnaw on."

"Oh, I assumed that would be the kind of dinner we might receive. I wasn't expecting her to be like your Betty Crocker. Do you think she'd share the liver or spleen? Those are the best."

"No." I shooed Duncan toward the parking lot, not caring *which* vehicle he got in. Ed and the Sylvans were approaching, and this was miles from being a *normal* conversation.

Duncan bowed to the group as he walked by them. I sighed. He couldn't even pass as normal when he kept his mouth shut.

"My truck," I called, when he paused, as if debating which vehicle to wait in. There weren't any metal detectors in there that he might be tempted to get out if the conversation went long.

Duncan waved in acknowledgment. The Sylvans looked back at him, and, yes, Rory's forehead *did* crease, as if he detected something odd about Duncan. Fortunately, I didn't sense more than a smidgen of a paranormal aura from him, less than from Bolin. Maybe druidic power varied as it was passed down through offspring. Or maybe Rory had done less to cultivate his talents, and it lay closer to dormancy.

Ed, a former sergeant major in the army, grunted a greeting when the group stopped in front of me on the walkway. A man of sixtyish with buzz-cut white hair, a broad build, and a granite jaw, he looked like he could still be in the army. As always, he wore a checkered flannel shirt instead of business attire. When life—and the apartment complex—had been running normally, I'd always appreciated his no-nonsense attitude, but now I braced myself for his bluntness.

"Hi, Bolin." I lifted a hand, trying not to let the wave appear tentative or nervous. "Ed. Mr. and Mrs. Sylvan."

Rory was a redhead, like his son, though his hair was fading with gray. He had round ruddy cheeks with a spattering of freckles above a trimmed beard and mustache that had gone fully gray. He wore a tailored suit with gold cuff links and a decorative tie bar that looked like a tree. A silent nod to his heritage?

The stern-faced Kashvi Sylvan wore a business suit with a head scarf and regarded me aloofly. That was, from what I recalled, her normal expression, so I didn't worry too much about it. Yet.

"Good afternoon, Ms. Valens," Kashvi said formally, taking the lead.

As I recalled, she represented the numbers and business half of the partnership—and perhaps the marriage. Rory might wear a suit now, but he'd been the handyman who'd fixed up their original rental properties. Until they'd amassed enough apartments and money to hire outsiders, they'd shared the responsibility of managing the tenants.

"We understand there's been trouble on the property lately," Rory said with a sympathetic smile. There was rarely anything stern about him, though I'd heard a misbehaving water heater could make him lose his temper and smack wrenches against walls.

"I told them everything I've seen," Bolin offered, the phrasing seeming to imply he hadn't mentioned lycanthropic intervention.

Ed wandered off, hands clasped behind his back, looking like he intended to do an inspection of the property. That was fine. I'd cleaned up all the messes and even removed all the moss from the roofs of the buildings. As long as no wolves wandered in from the greenbelt, he shouldn't find anything amiss.

"Crime has increased all through this area, I understand," Kashvi said, "but it's surprising that there have been multiple incidents at our apartments here in Shoreline."

"There have been a few things," I said, "but we've handled them."

"We?" Kashvi asked. "You're divorced, and your husband no longer helps out, correct?"

"He *never* helped out," I said before I could catch myself, certain that trashing my ex to my employers would make me look bad. "But, yes, he's gone. I meant, well, Bolin has been helpful."

I would explain Duncan if I had to, but that might involve admitting there was a guy living in the van in the parking lot. They would not approve of that.

Kashvi's eyebrows arched in surprise. "My son?"

Rory also appeared surprised, though he shot Bolin a pleased look.

Less pleased, Kashvi's expression grew sterner. "Our son assisted with the intervention of a dangerous crime?"

She turned to him, mouth opening for what might have been a forthcoming lecture.

"Just with the aftermath," I hurried to say, making her pause. It wasn't a lie. Other than tossing a glowing vial of whatever out to protect his SUV, Bolin hadn't been in any of the frays. "He was helpful about calling the police and dealing with all their questions while I cleaned up the messes and took photos for the insurance claims." And turned into a wolf and tore the intruders' throats out... I grimaced, keeping the last thought to myself.

"Ah, I see," Kashvi said.

Rory patted Bolin on the shoulder, still appearing more pleased that his son had helped than upset that he'd put himself in harm's way. Something told me Rory Sylvan would be okay with a vigilante crime-fighter dealing with issues in the neighborhood. He might even encourage his son to help someone with such an endeavor. Since he knew about the wolf case, and had been assisting with the research, he might know more about the goings-on here than his wife.

"We are concerned by the trend," Kashvi continued. "We have had this property for many years—decades—and we have watched Seattle grow from a sleepy one-industry town to a metropolis with all the problems associated with that, including crime. Never did we think this quaint suburb would have to deal with such things."

"It is distressing," I offered, not sure where she was going. "I could put up some more security cameras. One of the tenants suggested doorbell cameras, but that would be expensive to add to every unit." Maybe I shouldn't have mentioned it. The last thing I needed were *more* opportunities for cameras to capture footage of wolves darting around the complex and chewing on intruders. With my luck, I would change right in front of someone's doorbell and give it a full view of my naked butt turning furry.

"We appreciate your efforts to keep the tenants safe," Rory said, "and we're aware that you work hard and keep our costs way down by doing a lot of the repairs and maintenance yourself. This has become a very profitable property for us. It alone paid for Bolin's college tuition."

I reined in the snarky comment that came to mind, that I was glad me installing toilets and fixing dishwashers had allowed Bolin to dedicate himself to spelling-bee competitions and violin practice instead of working his way through college. Besides, Bolin was turning out to be a pretty decent guy, considering he was twenty-three and his parents paid for all his expenses. He could have been a snot.

"But," Rory continued, "we need to consider if it's time to sell this property and reinvest the profits elsewhere."

"Due to recent events," Kashvi said, "the insurance is increasing with the new year. It's increasing a great deal. As if it weren't egregious enough that the property taxes went up so much these past few years."

I rocked back, barely hearing her words after his. I had worried about them replacing me, but it had never crossed my mind that they would sell Sylvan Serenity Housing.

If they did, would I be able to continue working for the new owners? With the same deal that included my apartment? Or would they want to hire someone new? Someone young and perky with a college degree?

If new owners didn't want to keep me on, I would have to move after more than twenty years. Not only had I raised my kids here, but I'd put so much effort into maintaining the place these past decades that it felt like mine in a way. Even if there was more crime these days, it was a great location for commuting, and the acreage with the nearby trees made it far more peaceful than one would usually find in the city. Besides, it was my *territory*.

As if someone had punched me in the stomach, I realized I didn't want to leave, not unless it was because I'd finally reached my financial goals and could buy my own multifamily property. Even then, I didn't know if I would want to move. I might simply rent out the units of my new place and continue to work and live here.

If I had that option.

"We have not made up our mind yet," Rory said in an apologetic voice, watching the conflagration of emotions waltzing across my face.

"But it must be considered." Kashvi's no-nonsense tone suggested she didn't care that this was my territory and home and that I had feelings about it. For her, this would be a business decision, purely based on financial considerations.

"I understand," I said numbly.

And I did. That didn't mean it didn't disturb me. It *especially* disturbed me because much of the crime was my fault, or at least had occurred because I lived here. I didn't think the motorcycle gang had anything to do with me, but the rest...

I leaned forward and gripped my knees.

"We will not decide until after the holidays," Rory told me gently. "And we really do appreciate all the work you've done here over the years. If we sell, we'll make sure you receive an ample severance package, whether the new owners want to continue on with you or not."

"Thanks," I mumbled bleakly, afraid they had already made up their minds. They were talking about *the new owners* as if they had someone in mind.

Were there interested parties lined up for this place? Despite the news? I could see someone wanting to sell off chunks of the land, maybe breaking it off from the buildings for further development. Acreage this close to Seattle had to be worth a fortune these days.

Ed returned and nodded to the Sylvans. "From a cursory look, everything on the outside is in good repair, and the landscaping is well-tended. Any areas that criminals might lurk at night have been trimmed back from the well-lit walkways."

"I thought that would be the case," Rory told him.

Was that something they'd discussed? Debating if I was doing the work necessary to keep the place safe?

I straightened, trying not to feel indignant that my ability to manage the complex well might have been questioned.

"I told you overgrown bushes weren't the problem," Bolin murmured.

Ignoring him, Kashvi said, "We will keep you apprised on the situation, Ms. Valens." She lifted a hand, as if to take her leave, but paused. "How have the vacancies been lately?"

In light of the crime? And the newspaper articles?

I was relieved I could say, "We're full, with a waiting list."

I didn't mention that a quirky alchemist hoped to be put at the top of that waiting list. I definitely didn't mention we were now attracting tenants who kept ghostometers in their closets.

"Oh? That is a little surprising." Kashvi looked at her husband. "I expected that recent events..."

"It's a lot of work for people to move," Rory said blandly, glancing at me.

He might or might not know I was a werewolf, but he absolutely knew more about the paranormal aspect of recent problems than his wife. Of that, I was certain.

"Well, that is something at least," Kashvi said. "It will be a selling point if we can report that the vacancies are low."

"Nonexistent," Rory said.

"Indeed." Kashvi nodded to me. "Please carry on, Ms. Valens."

I mumbled an agreement but rubbed the back of my neck as the group walked away. I felt distressed but also... resolute. I didn't want to be forced to move and find a new job. No way were my dastardly cousins going to be the cause of that. I also didn't want them bilking people in the neighborhood out of money.

I lowered my arm and glowered into the trees, though I didn't sense them out there at the moment. Too bad. I was more than ready to deal with them. I would start with Mom and Lorenzo. This time, I intended to find a solution to Augustus and his siblings that was more permanent. If that meant transporting them to Canada and hurling them out the door of my moving truck, so be it.

As the Sylvans drove away, Duncan walked from his van to the passenger side of my truck and patted the door. Saying he was ready to visit the pack with me?

I nodded firmly and headed that way. As much as I hated relying on his help, I might need to in order to deal with my cousins. If he was willing to assist, I couldn't be too proud to accept.

"Ready to go see your mother?" Duncan joined me in the truck when I slid into the driver's seat.

"See her, yes, and also kick the butt of every werewolf who's stepped foot in Shoreline in the past year."

He raised his eyebrows. "*I've* stepped foot here."

I put the truck into gear. "You'd better gird your ass then."

10

THIS TIME, WHEN WE DROVE PAST MONROE AND INTO THE WOODS where my mom lived in her two-room log cabin, no surly were-wolves sprang out of the driveway to block us. I was almost surprised, but maybe Augustus was still lurking around Sylvan Serenity, waiting for a chance to raid my apartment and find the wolf case. Such an effort would prove futile since the artifact was in my glovebox, nestled atop two recently purchased bars of dark chocolate.

At the start of the driveway, magical items in the brush to either side pinged my senses. Whatever they were, they hadn't been there before. I couldn't see anything through the fern fronds, but I felt their presence.

"Your mother has added magical defenses," Duncan said.

"Is that what they are? She mentioned getting ready in case thieves shooting silver bullets raid her property again."

"Let's hope that, whatever the devices are, they don't attack helpful lone wolves who've done nothing to deserve having magic flung at them."

"Nothing? After you beat up my cousins, you pinned another

of my relatives to the wall of the cabin. I think you dislocated his shoulder."

"Those attacks were warranted."

"Do you want me to tell the magical devices that if they start pummeling you with sonic rays?"

"I would appreciate that, yes."

I glimpsed something glowing softly under a tree as the cabin came into view and wondered whom Mom knew who made and installed defensive magical artifacts. Maybe I could put some in around the apartment complex, though I would have to make sure the devices knew who to attack and who *not* to attack. After everything that had happened, I didn't need a magical landmine going off when one of the tenants' dogs peed on a bush.

When we arrived at the cabin, Mom's Jeep was parked in the driveway beside a twenty-year-old Subaru. I didn't know what Lorenzo drove but hoped that was his car. He wouldn't have a problem with me visiting, and he'd seemed okay with Duncan. At least, he hadn't *attacked* Duncan.

But when I knocked on the front door, an older woman answered, her gray hair dangling in a braid over her shoulder. I recognized the wise wolf who'd tended Emilio, removing the silver bullet that had lodged in his torso, and concern tightened my throat. Rosaria was her name, I remembered, though I hadn't had cause to interact with her often in my youth.

"Is Mom okay?" I blurted for my greeting.

"Good evening, Luna. And..." Rosaria looked toward Duncan. "Lone wolf who smashed Rocco against the wall of the cabin."

She'd seen that? She must have been peering out the window at the time.

"Duncan. And I'm sorry you had to witness such violence." He bowed apologetically to her.

"Werewolves are not bothered by violence. More tedious was setting his dislocated shoulder later. He was a dreadful patient."

"He was a dreadful opponent as well." Duncan nodded. "So very surly."

"Yes, that sounds right." Rosaria smiled faintly at him before looking at me again.

I leaned forward, more worried about Mom than Rocco.

"She is... not in the best of conditions," Rosaria admitted quietly. "She is a somewhat surly patient herself, refusing the human treatments and medication and rarely accepting even the tinctures and potions I offer to ease her pain."

"I don't want my pain eased," came Mom's voice from the kitchen. "I *like* my pain. It tells me I'm still alive."

"Surly," Rosaria said again.

"She's proud," I offered. "She always was."

Rosaria sniffed. "Proudly surly."

I spread my arms, unable to argue with that. "Is there anything *I* can do? I've wondered..." I looked at Duncan. "Is it possible a magical potion might be able to help her? We know an alchemist."

"One who specializes in werewolf pharmacology?"

"Uhm." I'd had no idea there was such a thing as werewolf pharmacology. "She has a lot of books on a variety of topics."

Rosaria pressed her lips together in a thin line. I decided it wouldn't be a point in Rue's favor if I mentioned that she could make potions that *sublimated* werewolf powers.

"She's human with some magical blood," I said, "but I don't know what her background is."

"I do not think it likely a potion would have the power to stop the spread of the Taint and destroy the corrupted cells."

"The Taint? Is that your term for cancer? That's what Mom has, right?"

"That is what the human doctors call it, yes."

"And there's no cure that she would accept?" A thought came to me. "Do you know about her medallion? That couldn't help heal her, could it?"

To be a treasured family heirloom handed down from mother to daughter over the centuries, it surely had to do something more than glow brightly.

"I do know about it, yes. Your mother never disclosed its powers to me, but I had the same thought and asked her to wear it when she rests. It hasn't yet healed her, unfortunately, but it does seem to soothe her somewhat. From what I *have* learned of its power, it's meant more to protect the pack and our territory than heal illnesses or injuries. And its power is diminished currently since the matching medallion disappeared."

"There's another one?" I asked before remembering the history Mom had given when she'd first shown her artifact to me. She'd mentioned that hers was for female werewolves and one that had been designed for males had been lost.

"There was once, one that the alpha male usually wore. It disappeared long ago. It may not even have made it to the New World with the pack. I am uncertain. Your mother may know more, but, either way, I fear the medallion won't cure the Taint. We can only do what we can to ease her pain." Rosaria looked over her shoulder into the cabin, her voice growing louder and sterner when she added, "Inasmuch as a dreadful patient such as she will allow a wise wolf to ease her pain."

"Let my daughter in, Rosaria," Mom called. "I sense that the lone wolf is with her, and I wish to meet him."

"You need rest, Umbra."

"If I rest any more, I'll get bedsores, and you'll have to rub one of your creams all over me. The one that smells like dying skunks, perhaps."

"Dreadful patient," Rosaria repeated, shaking her head as she descended the stairs from the porch.

"It sounds like Mom's in a good mood and wants to see you." I waved for Duncan to follow me.

"That's a good mood?" he asked, though he sounded more amused than concerned or reluctant at meeting my mother.

"I didn't hear her throw anything across the room."

"My diminished state makes throwing heavy objects more difficult these days." In her room, Mom sat propped up in bed with a book, her long white hair loose about her shoulders and what looked like a whiskey tumbler on the table next to her. A twist of lemon floated on the ice cubes, and the amber liquid inside did have the sharp smell of alcohol.

"Aren't sick people supposed to drink orange juice?" I stepped inside, not sure if she wanted Duncan to come into her bedroom or to meet him in the living area.

"Juice is cloyingly sweet." Mom made a face. "I like a drink that kicks you in the throat a few times on the way down."

"She is a tough lady," Duncan remarked from the doorway.

Mom squinted at him.

"Mom, this is Duncan, a lone wolf from... the Old World." I couldn't share the tale he'd given me in confidence, but that didn't seem too much to offer. He'd told me that much long before he'd admitted to the rest.

"I could have guessed that."

"From my melodious accent?" Duncan bowed to her.

"You emanate power like a sun, have the chiseled physique of an alpha, and have abs taut enough to deflect bullets."

Duncan's jaw drooped open. "I... hadn't realized my abs could indicate my birthplace."

"All the old-world werewolves I met in my youth were more impressive than the pups born here today." Mom waved vaguely to indicate our pack's territory, or maybe all of America. "More impressive and more dangerous."

She leveled an assessing gaze at Duncan.

"Maybe having their abs pelted with bullets makes them irritable." Duncan rubbed his stomach as he made a face.

Mom looked at me. "He's goofier than you are."

"I'm not that goofy," I said. "But *he* tries to disarm people with affable charm."

"Before he ruthlessly slays them? And I'll remind you that you put tinsel on my tail one year during the human winter holiday."

"I haven't forgotten. And Duncan thus far hasn't ruthlessly slain me, so that speaks well of him, I should think."

"Quite," Duncan murmured, though his eyes grew dark for a moment. Was he thinking of the control device and how he'd attacked me? I hoped that as long as we kept our distance from Abrams, Duncan wouldn't be susceptible to its power.

I mulled over a way to shift the topic to my cousins, but Mom wasn't done speaking with Duncan.

"What are your intentions toward my daughter?"

Duncan and I blinked in surprise.

He recovered first. "I've been attempting to woo her into my lair for a healthy adult frolic, but she's thus far evaded my advances."

I groaned. I'd always heard Europeans were more open about sex, but there were some things one shouldn't bring up with a woman's mother. And *my* mother didn't look amused.

"My daughter doesn't need to frolic like a horny teenager," she said. "She needs a suitable mate to breed healthy werewolf pups with before her fertile period ends."

My second groan was even louder, and my hand came up to cover my rapidly heating face. By all the howling wolves in the forest, there were also things one shouldn't discuss with a guy one had just met. Even *I* hadn't known Duncan long enough to bring up *pups*.

"We haven't discussed that possibility yet." Duncan looked at me, his eyebrows up.

"No, we have not. And we're not going to." I faced Mom. "I *have* children, *grown* children. And I'm forty-five. I'm too old to have more."

She lifted her eyes toward the wooden ceiling planks, as if I were the dimmest of her offspring. "I already told you, Luna. Werewolves are fertile longer than humans. Nature intended that. In our quests for dominance and quality hunting grounds, we kill each other off left and right. We're much more aggressive than our unmagical lupine kin. Further, the threat we represent makes us targets for other species as well. As I'm sure you've noticed. Our creators gave us a long span of fertility so we'd have the ability to have numerous pups to replenish our species."

"That's fine, Mom, but—"

"And your *human* babies are..." She flicked her hand, as if she were tossing garbage over her shoulder. "Inconsequential."

Indignation and anger on their behalf made me lift my chin and snap, "They're anything but that. Their *father* may be a loser, but they're good kids. Austin is serving in the military as we speak, ready to defend this nation in time of war."

"This human nation." Mom flicked her hand again. "Werewolves do not recognize arbitrary borders created by human conflicts and politics. To us, it doesn't matter which of them thinks they rule over this land. *We* claim this territory and will defend it."

"Augustus is claiming *more* than the territory the pack has historically patrolled," I said, jumping on the chance to move the topic away from my fertility. "Do you know about his mafia habits, Mom?"

She frowned at me. "Mafia?"

I explained the bartender and convenience-store owners and how Augustus was demanding monthly *taxes* from people. "He apparently claims it's for their protection, but he's a shitty protector."

"Given his fighting prowess, I wouldn't trust him to protect a goldfish bowl," Duncan murmured.

Mom waved a hand. "Bella coddled and over-praised her children when they were growing up. Against my wishes, she even fed them substandard fare." She curled her lip. "She kept *Fruit Hoops* in her cupboard."

"Froot Loops, you mean?"

"Breakfast candies for children. *Human* children. Werewolves consume meat, bone, and organs for breakfast. For *all* meals."

"I've seen you eat dark chocolate, Mom. I know you're not completely carnivorous."

"A tiny amount of sweet indulgence is permissible after a nutritionally satisfying meal has been consumed. Not after *Fruit Hoops*." Never had someone mispronounced the popular breakfast cereal so scathingly.

I didn't mention that I had, on numerous occasions, given in to my sons' whining at the store and purchased those as well as Cocoa Pebbles for them. That would only lead Mom to think them even more inferior.

Duncan scratched his jaw. "So, we can blame malnourishment as a child for your cousin's brutish behavior as an adult?" he asked me.

"It sounds like it was a collection of things."

"He also grew up without a father," Mom said. "As you did, Luna. This is not atypical in werewolf society though. Often, it's only the alphas who stick around, leading the pack as well as their household. Your father would have been an excellent alpha if he'd stayed." She looked wistfully toward the window.

I cleared my throat, more interested in the present than the past. "I want to stop Augustus, Mom. I don't visit downtown Seattle and that bar often, but nobody deserves to be strongarmed by werewolves. And Shoreline is... my territory."

I didn't necessarily consider more than the apartment complex *my territory*, but she would understand the notion.

"You will challenge him?" she asked.

"Do I need to? He's dragging the pack's name through the mud. I thought you and Lorenzo and maybe the other elders might... kick him out. Maybe kick *all* of them out." I waved toward the forest to imply the rest of Augustus's bully siblings.

Mom didn't answer right away, only gazing steadily at me. Why did I have the feeling she'd wanted me to answer her question with *yes, I would challenge him*? Had Augustus been the only one making trouble, I would have been willing, but he hadn't thus far allowed me to face him one-on-one. The word honor didn't seem to be in his vocabulary.

"The other elders might be swayed by Lorenzo or the arbiter to take such action," Mom said, "but your cousins are young and strong, so there might be deaths if the issue were forced. If that is to be, it's to be, but I believe the arbiter would require evidence of their wrongdoing before choosing that route. In addition to the possibility of deaths, to ask so many to leave would diminish the power of the pack."

"They *can't* be adding that much value."

"They hunt and patrol our territory."

"*More* than our territory," I muttered before catching myself, worried Mom would point out that I'd been away from the pack for too long to include myself in that *our*. "What kind of evidence would I need to present?"

I didn't have any idea who the arbiter was these days. Had there even been one in the pack when I'd been young? I couldn't remember.

"Something convincing." Mom got out of bed, clasped her hands behind her back, and walked to the window. "I have heard that Augustus is separated from his wife at this time. He has acquired a large home on the lake in Sammamish, and it is reputedly quite lavish for a werewolf. For *anyone*."

"He's probably using the money he collects in *taxes* to pay for it."

"That may be a possibility. Several of your cousins also spend time there, but they, I believe, have only part-time employment in the human world, so they may not be contributing to the rent."

"Then Augustus is going to have a hard time making the payments if someone stops him from extorting people." I touched my chest.

"Likely so, but I will not shed a tear. A werewolf does not need a luxury human home." Mom sniffed disdainfully. "Until recently, our kind usually lived in caves." She curled a lip as she considered the log walls of her cabin. "We have grown soft, I fear. I blame the waning of magic in the world, but perhaps we've at least partially done it to ourselves."

"It's probably the effect of the Fruit Hoops," Duncan said.

Mom shook her head and returned to her bed, leaning against the pillows again. "Do what you must, my daughter. Just know that it is unlikely the pack will turn against those boys without evidence of their wrongdoing."

"I understand."

"And be careful. Augustus is a brute but also a schemer. There's one in every family."

"Every werewolf family, maybe."

"Our kind tend toward orneriness." Mom gazed thoughtfully at me. "Lorenzo and I did tell Augustus to leave you be, but I am not surprised he has gone against our wishes. He has tested Lorenzo often and made it clear he desires leadership of the pack for himself. Lorenzo doesn't care whether he leads or not and has only stepped in since we had a succession of alphas and no clear leadership for a time, but he will not back down to an upstart."

"Good."

"And, as of yet, neither Augustus nor any of your cousins has challenged him in open combat."

"Because they're not good fighters," Duncan suggested. "They're strong, but they lack agility and cunning."

Mom's thoughtful gaze shifted to him. "I suspect you find that true of *most* wolves you fight. Most anyones. Were you to seek to mate with my daughter, I would grant my approval. With you, she would have superior offspring."

"*Mom*... Look, I get that you're probably thinking about your own mortality and trying to set things straight with your legacy right now, but I'm not having any more children."

"You must. Your blood is greater than that of my other offspring. You are the only child I had with your father, and his blood... He was magnificent."

"If I challenge Augustus," I said sturdily, determined to keep the conversation on track. "And things get... heated..." I thought of the times my savage wolf instincts had taken over completely and I'd killed. "Would you forgive that? Would Aunt Bella?"

What if the whole family turned against me? Before, when I'd left and been taking the sublimation potion, they'd all ignored me, for the most part, but this could be worse. They might openly hunt me to drive me out of Washington altogether.

"She might not forgive you," Mom said, "but you know what I believe. Only the strong survive. That is the way of the wolf."

"Yeah. I guess I figured you would feel that way."

"Were the arbiter and the other elders to decide he and the others had to go, Bella would have to accept that or leave with them."

"So... getting evidence to condemn him should be my first strategy."

That idea struck me as more appealing than possibly killing a relative, even a live-by-the-fang-die-by-the-fang werewolf relative, but would it solve the problem? Or would it start a war within the pack? If Augustus and his siblings challenged Lorenzo and ended up in charge of the Savagers...

"Deal with him, one way or another, if you can," Mom said. "It might ultimately bring harmony to the pack. There is tension now between the elders and the youths. Such is not uncommon among our kind, but it has been years without resolution and grows tedious. If Augustus or Marco or one of the others desires to be our leader, they should challenge Lorenzo openly. Instead, they mutter and scheme. More than once, I have been concerned that they would plot his demise through some seeming accident rather than challenging him openly and nobly."

"Like they'd cut the brake lines in his car or something?" I could imagine it. The turds.

Mom took a long drink from the whiskey glass. Most of the ice cubes had melted while we spoke.

"I fear that is possible," she said after draining it. "I would miss Lorenzo, as he has become a faithful companion to me these past years. He is also a stabilizing force for the pack."

"I'm glad he's taking care of you, Mom."

She squinted at me. "I am not so old and infirm that I am unable to care for myself."

"I'm certain that's true."

"Two nights ago, I took down a buck by myself."

"You're a fit and virile female wolf."

"You're humoring me. Come closer so I can slap you for your impertinence."

Since I caught a smile in her eyes, I didn't think she meant it.

"I'd better not," I said. "Duncan defends me from threats."

"Does he?" Mom looked more approving than concerned.

He bowed again to her. "With my bulletproof abs, my lady."

I snorted. That wasn't a body part I'd yet seen him sling at my cousins.

"Good," Mom said. "Step outside for a moment. Refill this while you're there." She lifted the empty whiskey glass and held it toward him.

"With orange juice, right?" Duncan accepted it with a smirk.

"Your impertinence is also deserving of slaps," she said sternly, but, yes, that *was* a smile in her eyes.

"I get that a lot." He lifted the glass, then walked out, closing the door to give us the privacy Mom wanted.

I eyed her warily, afraid my fertility would come up again.

Instead, Mom opened her nightstand drawer and withdrew the black-velvet-covered box that held the medallion. I tensed, afraid she believed her death was coming soon and she meant to give it to me now.

"There is a cave not far from here." Mom opened the box, and the golden wolf-head medallion with its equally golden chain glowed softly.

I remembered how it had blazed when I'd touched it in front of Lord Abrams and Radomir.

"Several generations ago, the first of our pack to enter into and claim this territory left paintings and sprinkled potions and other magic about the cave. It has been a sacred place for a long time for the females of our line. Had you stayed and mated with an alpha, I would have shared its location with you many years ago. Much of the lore has been lost, and I do not know what all the paintings signify. I do know that this—" Mom lifted the medallion from its resting place, "—glows more strongly there than I have seen it do anywhere else. I always felt some secret was in the cave and that, if discovered, it would teach us to more fully use the medallion's power to strengthen our pack and protect it from outsiders."

"It does seem like the pack needs more protection these days."

Her eyelids drooped. "Some of those men with silver bullets returned. They did not leave their vehicles and remained on the road, but they used binoculars to peer in this direction. I believe they sensed the newly placed magical defenses near the driveway and decided not to attack at this time, but they are still after this." She jingled the medallion chain.

"I'm sorry."

Between his grenades and his raw strength, Duncan had nearly destroyed the security forces at the potion factory, but Radomir was probably wealthy enough to hire brutes by the dozen. Or the *hundred*. Maybe there was, even now, a "Thugs Wanted" sign on the community board at El Gato Mágico.

Sooner or later, I would have to deal with Abrams and Radomir if I wanted their subordinates to stop trying to steal werewolf artifacts, but I could only handle one set of evildoers at a time.

"Before you go, I want you to visit the cave. See if you, perhaps with that one's help—" Mom pointed her chin toward the door, "—can learn more about the ancient magic within it."

I was more interested in handling my cousins than going spelunking, but, after disappearing from her life for so many years, I owed it to my mother to obey her wishes. All except the creating-more-offspring one, anyway.

"It's possible that what you learn there will assist you with facing your cousins," Mom offered, as if she knew my thoughts. "It may also help you figure out why those people want this." She held the medallion out to me.

I drew back. "You're keeping that until you pass, right?"

"I will, but take it for tonight. The cave will respond to it. You may learn more if you carry it inside."

"Okay." I accepted the medallion, though its cool weight in my hands made me uneasy, as if this exchange were signaling Mom's death. I vowed to bring it back before going home. "You say this cave is nearby?"

"Yes." She delved into her drawer again and withdrew a pen and a journal. "I will draw you a map."

"Okay," I repeated.

"Take the old-world werewolf with you."

"Duncan."

"Yes."

"You trust him now?" I asked.

She hadn't when he'd first come with me to visit her. She'd warned me to watch out for him.

"Trust? No. But, as I said, he is an ideal male with whom to produce offspring. Despite being slightly past his prime, I believe his virility will ensure his seed takes with only a few matings."

"My exact thoughts when I met him." I couldn't keep the sarcasm out of my tone. I wished she would knock this off.

"If only you were in earnest." Mom looked up from her map drawing to shake her head sadly at me. "I have hope that you will see the truth. I believe he is drawn to you."

"It's my boobs."

I expected another head shake, but Mom nodded. "The females in our line have always had appealing anatomy."

I snorted, accepted the map when she tore it out of her journal, and opened the door. Duncan stood there, the refilled whiskey glass in hand. With his hearing, he'd probably caught every word of the discussion. He set the glass on the bedside table, then walked out with me, glancing at the medallion and piece of paper.

"My mom offered me a quest," I said. "Do you want to come?"

"You drove, so I think that's required."

I considered the map, the directions starting at the back door of the cabin. "This looks like a walking quest."

"Ah. I always enjoy an amble with a fine lady."

"Good. Thanks."

"Since you are seeking a mission," he said as we headed into the woods, "it's kind of the world to keep offering them to you."

"I suppose."

"Will you need a mask and cape for your mother's quest?"

"I think capes are optional at sacred caves."

11

TWILIGHT SETTLED IN AS WE PADDED THROUGH THE WOODS BEHIND Mom's home, heading toward a gully that would eventually lead into state land. Since I hadn't grown up in the cabin, I didn't know the area that well. I attempted to pull up a map on my phone to use alongside her sketch, but the poor reception made it take a long time to load.

"It'll be hard to see if we continue in human form." Duncan walked at my side as we navigated over logs and between ferns.

Apparently, Mom hadn't visited her sacred cave often enough to wear a path in the earth.

"It's hard to hold a map in wolf form," I said.

"True."

I slanted him a sidelong look. "Can you hold things while in the two-legged form?"

Duncan hadn't gone into details on that, and I didn't know if he'd chosen to become the bipedfuris at the potion factory, or if Lord Abrams pressing buttons on his control device had caused that to happen. Since I was incapable of turning into that, I had no idea how the magic decided whether it was time for a person to become a wolf or the classical two-legged werewolf from the old days.

"Yes, but the claws tend to shred paper, and I can't fully grasp words—reading. For a lover of literature, that's alarming. If I'm to change, I prefer to be a wolf."

"Is that actually true or are you saying that because you think I find your lupine form less alarming?"

"My *lupine* form didn't try to keep you from escaping that compound." Duncan grimaced and swiped his fingers through the air to mimic clawed paws.

That hadn't answered my question, but we had to focus on climbing down into the gully, rocks and earth slipping under our feet, and I didn't press him. Water trickled along the bottom, gurgling as it meandered past mossy boulders and aged stumps. According to Mom's drawing, we needed to follow the waterway until the sides of the gully grew rocky with steeper slopes. At that point, we would find a cave among the crags.

Near the bottom, Duncan stopped me with a light touch. He gazed upstream into the deepening gloom. It felt much later than the five p.m. that my phone reported, but we were nearing the winter solstice, and the days were short.

"I sense something in that direction." Duncan pointed with his chin. "Multiple somethings, and... more."

"More than somethings?"

"Quite."

"Whatever it is, it's probably not dangerous. Mom wouldn't have sent me into a den of vipers."

Duncan kept gazing into the gloom and didn't comment.

"Vipers are in short supply in Western Washington anyway," I said. "The worst we have are garter snakes."

"There are other dangers." After contemplating me briefly, he started removing his clothes.

"Do you want me to change too?"

If he could sense the magic of the cave, we could probably find it without a map, but the calm evening didn't have my skin pricking with the need to change. Unless a threat presented itself, I didn't know if I could.

"Not unless you want to. I'll lead." Clothes removed and draped over a boulder, Duncan stepped to the side, the change sweeping over him.

In the dark, I couldn't see much of his nudity—the physical attributes that my mom had praised—but that was fine. I hadn't come out here to ogle anyone. My senses did perk with awareness as his power fluctuated along with his body, growing more lupine, more noticeable. He dropped to all fours as he became the wolf.

Though I hadn't admitted it to him, I was relieved he hadn't turned into the bipedfuris. It might have been because he'd lost control and attacked me in that form, but it might also have been because two-legged werewolves weren't anything I'd grown up around. It was the stuff of legend, and, in this age, seemed closer to a monster than the noble wolf. I would have been uneasy walking beside him that way.

Duncan, the silhouette of his pointed ears just visible in the lingering daylight, looked at me, as if he knew my thoughts, then padded upstream. I hurried to catch up, resting a hand on his back, the cool lushness of his thick fur comforting. He was the wolf, nothing else. Nothing that was a danger to me.

Soon, I sensed what he had. Magic. Multiple kinds, as he'd said, though all coming from the same general area.

Some reminded me of artifacts but others felt like magical beings. Would this cave be guarded? Maybe it wouldn't be as safe to visit as I'd assumed.

Duncan paused, his head cocking as he looked upslope. The walls had steepened with great trees growing at the top. Their evergreen branches stretched over the gully, almost as if intentionally hiding this place from above. No satellites or helicopters would have a view down here.

A pair of red dots glowed from between two trees, and I twitched. Eyes.

I hadn't turned on a flashlight, nor was any other illumination around, nothing that could have reflected off eyes to make them appear red. Those were truly glowing.

I remembered the night Duncan and I had battled dogs and wolves that someone—I suspected Augustus—had sent to attack us. Could my cousins be in the area?

For the first time, my skin heated, magic sweeping through my veins. The hint of a threat was stirring my blood, offering the ability to change.

Not certain if it was wise, I attempted to tamp down the magic. Since I was holding Mom's map and wearing her medallion, I would prefer to remain in human form. A werewolf artifact *should* change with me, rather than disappearing into the ether like my clothes, but the possibility that I could lose a magical heirloom that had been handed down for generations scared me.

Duncan's head turned toward another slope. Partway up, a different set of eyes looked toward us. When he focused on them, whatever animal possessed them darted off, the foliage rustling. A fox? Or would there be mongrel dogs out here? The animal hadn't seemed large enough to be a wolf.

I folded the map and put it in my pocket. It was too dark to read anyway unless I pulled out my phone's flashlight. Instead, I wrapped my hand around the medallion, willing it to guide me.

Silver light leaked out between my fingers, shining into the gloom and reflecting off the water of the stream. Power emanated from the medallion, warming my hand, and coursing through me, almost *infusing* me with even greater magic than was inherent in my blood. It reminded me of the witch's locket that Duncan and I had found, but this had much more power. I had the urge to let my head fall back and soak it in.

I felt Duncan's gaze upon me, and he shifted closer, his furry shoulder against me. Drawn to me? He'd said he was before, but it might have been the magic of the medallion that pulled him in, nothing about me.

But his eyes were locked to mine, not to the artifact. A flush of warmth swept through me that didn't have anything to do with magic. For some reason, my mom's words came to mind about him being an appropriate mate. She'd been too blunt, and far too interested in me having more children, but a part of me was glad she approved of Duncan. Because I wanted him. It hadn't always been wise—maybe it *still* wasn't wise—but I had all along.

I blew out a breath and looked away from Duncan's steady gaze to focus on the way ahead. Maybe it was good that we were in different forms and wouldn't be tempted by each other's allure. Not unless he changed back or I took my wolf form.

"Maybe later," I murmured.

Like moonlight, the medallion's illumination cast the world in shades of light and dark instead of allowing one to see color, but I did notice something glowing blue near a tree stump. Mushrooms. They registered as very faintly magical to my senses.

Duncan pulled his gaze from me and continued forward. I stayed close to him.

So far, I didn't get the feeling that the glowing-eyed animals were warning us to stay away, but would that change? I imagined a pack guarding the cave entrance.

When we reached the rockier area, the silver light beaming over mossy boulders, the ground and ferns strewn with damp fallen leaves, I felt stronger magic coming from the steep slope on the opposite side of the stream. It was almost a cliff, long tree roots dangling down from twenty feet above. A dark crack might have been a cave entrance.

Light on his paws, Duncan hopped over the stream and headed toward the cliff. A shadow moved on a boulder near it, and glowing red eyes stared at him. Something growled. It did sound like a fox.

He growled back, and it sprang away. It leaped up boulders to the top of the cliff, the silver light catching its bushy tail before it disappeared.

When Duncan reached the crack, he looked back at me. Waiting.

Was that the right spot? The entrance was only a few feet high and a couple of feet wide, barely enough for him to slip through as a wolf. I'd expected something larger and more grandiose. But I could sense more magic inside, so I didn't hesitate to hop over the stream. I had to lower into a crouch, almost on my hands and knees, to squeeze through the crack after Duncan.

It would have been easier as a wolf, and I almost reconsidered, certain that with all the magic in the area and more coming from the medallion I could take that form. But I might forget what we sought then and be lured off by the desire to hunt.

Soon, the cave grew wider and taller, enough that I could stand fully, though the lumpy ground, the rocks slick with algae or who knew what, made doing so a challenge.

More glowing mushrooms grew in clumps, and patches of moss or some kind of similar vegetation also glowed, green instead of blue. They congregated near a pool that emanated magic of its own. The water was dark, though, with no hint of illumination, save that of my medallion reflecting off the surface. Something fuzzy carpeting the roof of the cave created a white glow up there. This whole place was magical.

Duncan padded forward and took a few licks from the pool.

"I'm not sure that's a safe place for a drink," I said.

Unlike the stream outside, the pool was still and might have been stagnant. Even if it was a spring with fresh water flowing in, all the glowing growth around it made me think of radiation. Then there was also the magic that welled within the pool.

When Duncan looked back at me, his eyes glowed red.

I swore and jumped back, alarm surging through me. Again, my blood heated my body with the promise that I could change if I needed to.

I swallowed. Did I need to? Duncan merely gazed at me. Other than his eyes, nothing about him changed, and, even as I watched, they faded back to their normal brown.

"Yeah," I croaked. "Definitely don't drink the water."

His tongue lolled out, and his eyes crinkled with humor.

"Maybe that's the reason the wildlife around here has red eyes." I wondered if they were drawn to the pool over other sources of water. "Do you think it's linked to the dogs and wolves that attacked us in town? Could Augustus know about this place? I've heard of some werewolves that can control other animals, though I wouldn't have guessed my cousin had that talent. It's more of a wise wolf kind of thing, a gift those with the power to heal and manipulate nature have. But maybe he knows about this place and learned to use it to his advantage."

I imagined Augustus bottling some of that water to take and give to animals. Did it do more than turn their eyes red? Maybe it made them more susceptible to commands or other types of magic.

Duncan sniffed a mossy patch by the water, then looked at me again. With significance in his eyes? I wasn't sure, but when I stepped closer, the medallion's light playing over the moss, I noticed a couple of scuffed spots where chunks had been torn away, revealing dirt beneath. Because someone had been in here recently?

"My mom said something about cave paintings," I said, reminded of why she'd sent me here. "And thought I might learn something more about the medallion and how to draw upon its power."

Duncan sat on his haunches, as if to say he would wait patiently for me to figure things out.

"You're a good companion."

His tongue lolled out again as he lifted his snout. *Obviously,* his expression seemed to say.

Smiling, I held the medallion away from my chest and directed it toward the dirt and stone walls of the cave. Before the silver light shone onto them, they appeared bare, save for a few black squiggles that may have been made with a piece of charred wood. But when the medallion's illumination beamed upon the stone, a number of outlines appeared. They were of paw prints, *wolf* paw prints. Of different sizes, they glowed back at me with the same moonlight-like illumination as the medallion.

The ceiling also glowed with paintings. Wolf heads looked down upon us from above. At the back of the cave, a pack of wolves chased a deer behind a boulder. It was the paw prints that called to me though, pulling my gaze back to them.

One of medium size—might that have been a match for my own foot, were I in my wolf form?—drew me, and I lifted a hand. Some certainty told me that this was what my mother had wanted me to see. Also, I sensed that touching it might give me answers.

I rounded the pool, careful not to step in the water, and climbed over the uneven ground, picking my way past rock formations that jutted upward to impede progress.

When I laid my hand over the paw, a startling surge of power rushed into me. It hurled me backward with the force of a hurricane gale.

Silver light flared so brightly that it blinded me. I flailed as power propelled my body through the air until it dropped me to the ground, my head clunking against a rock. The illumination brightened and brightened, its intensity overwhelming me, and I lost consciousness.

12

THE BRILLIANT LIGHT FADED, AND I FOUND MYSELF IN A DIM FOREST, rain falling from a gray sky as I looked at my mother's medallion. It had been around my neck, but now it hung from a tree branch, the wolf on the front howling and glowing faintly. I walked toward it, but the forest around me disappeared.

Suddenly, I was in a sunlit market with hundreds of dark-skinned people around stalls where street vendors hawked everything from scarves to grilled meat on skewers to glass art and carved wooden knickknacks.

An out-of-place pale-skinned man in a safari hat meandered past the stalls, a distracted look in his eyes as if he were daydreaming. A child pickpocket reached for him, but the man had the wherewithal to swat the probing hand away. He turned toward a stall, and I gaped with surprise. It was my ex-husband, Chad. And on a table in the stall lay a hodgepodge of knickknacks, including the ivory wolf case.

Hell, was that *really* how he'd found it? I'd assumed he'd been lying, that something so valuable wouldn't have been for sale in a street market. What about that story about how it had come from a vampire's castle? No, Radomir had said it had been *stolen* from the vampire's castle. If that was true, it had taken a long journey before Chad found it.

His eyes locked onto the case and sharpened, and he twitched, as if a hand had slapped his cheek, knocking him out of a trance. Gesticulating and waving American money, he negotiated with the vendor. A twenty-dollar bill was all it took, and he walked away with the prize.

A sense of satisfaction emanated from him. No... it seemed like that feeling came from the *case*. But in the weeks I'd been close to it, it hadn't given off any emotions, none that I'd detected.

This was a dream or vision, I reminded myself. Not reality.

The view blurred and changed to show Chad on a ship, sailing back to the Pacific Northwest where he would store the case in our apartment. Once more, the view blurred, and there was Chad again, standing on a dock stretching out from a sandy beach with tropical vegetation behind it. In the first vision, he'd had a beard. Now, he was clean-shaven and a couple of years older.

Duncan stood in front of him, looking just as he did now. Again, there was gesticulating. The vision didn't offer any words, any hint about what their conversation was, but if Duncan had told the truth, they were discussing him going to get the case.

I sensed that satisfaction again. From Duncan? No, it seemed to come from the case. Maybe all this was from the vision itself. Which originated... Where? In the cave? The paw print drawings? The magic that a powerful werewolf had infused in this area generations ago?

The last vision I received was of Duncan sailing out of the tropics. Toward the Pacific Northwest and the same place where the case had been stored. And not far from where Mom's wolf medallion existed.

Though no words ever floated into my mind during the vision, the magic somehow conveyed the idea that the bringing together of the artifacts had been orchestrated. By whom? The power of the moon? Of destiny? I hoped not the weirdos in the potion factory.

Blackness replaced the visions, and I slept.

What seemed like seconds later but might have been hours, I woke to night's embrace, the cloudy sky visible overhead, though dark branches largely blocked it. My head should have hurt—I remembered hitting it—and I was aware of a swollen lump, but it didn't bother me. After the visions, or whatever those had been, I felt... *good*. As if that magic had infused me with health and vigor. Since it had also tossed me on my ass, I couldn't be entirely grateful.

I'd been knocked out inside the cave though. How had I gotten out in the gully? Since I was lying on my back, there should have been cold rocks or damp earth underneath me, but I felt the warmth of someone else pressed against me. Duncan, I sensed, his scent and his aura comfortable.

He'd returned to his human form, sitting with me lying half in his lap, his arms around me, his back to a boulder. When I shifted a hand to touch his arm, I found him clothed. Since he'd been in his wolf form when I'd been... What *had* happened to me? Some kind of mental overload that had knocked me out? And for how long? It was still night, but that didn't mean much. This time of year, twelve hours could have passed, and it would remain dark.

"You're not naked," I mumbled, my mouth dry.

I had a feeling I'd been out for a lot longer than a few minutes. The memory of the visions remained, sharper and more permanent than dreams.

"If that's disappointment in your voice, perhaps I erred in fetching my clothing before returning to protect you."

"Is that what you're doing now?"

"It is."

"I feel cuddled." I couldn't complain. Being in his arms was better than being sprawled askew on the rocky cave floor or lying in a bed of dew-damp ferns.

"A good man knows how to protect *and* gently cuddle his lady."

"That must be why my mother kept suggesting you as a mate."

"You think so? She seemed overly concerned with the power of magic within me and if I'd pass it on to any children we might have."

His voice was light, and he didn't sound put off, but I couldn't tell for sure. The words made me wonder if Mom's idea of using him for breeding stock had offended him. It would have offended *me*.

"She noticed your abs too," I said, hoping to keep the conversation light.

"That was more alarming than flattering."

"Are you speaking the truth, Duncan Calderwood? Something tells me you'd find being ogled even by octogenarians flattering."

"Hm."

"I thought so."

"I'd prefer being ogled by you and would be happy to make my bulletproof abs available for the purpose. Unfortunately, you were unconscious when I shifted back into my naked human form."

"Something more pressing occupied me."

"Yeah." He brushed a lock of hair away from my forehead. "Are you well? I didn't get there in time to catch you when you fell, and you cracked your skull on a boulder. I didn't *expect* you to fall after touching a rock."

"It was startling to me too." I reached up, touched the lump, and found it tender, even if it wasn't giving me the splitting headache it probably should have.

"I wasn't sure what to do. Your medallion glowed toward the cave wall, and those paw paintings kind of glowed back with light that surrounded you. I lifted you off the ground, figuring I could carry you back to your mother's cabin, but the magic intensified and sizzled all over my skin. Enough to be painful. It seemed like a warning and resisted when I tried to take you outside, so I left you in there. After making sure you were breathing, I ran to the cabin and let your mother know what was happening. She only nodded, like she'd expected it, and said you would be fine. I... got a little pushy with her and might have forcefully demanded that she call the wise wolf to come check on you."

"Did it work?"

"I don't know. She's not an easily intimidated woman."

"No. She was—is—a somewhat difficult mother too."

"I expect so. I was worried about leaving you alone for long, especially after seeing all those animals with the red eyes, so I hurried back."

I thought about pointing out that *he'd* briefly had glowing red eyes after lapping at the pool, but he continued on before I could.

"By the time I returned, the paws had stopped glowing, and so had your medallion. You were alone in the dark in there. I'm glad nothing happened. That fox was outside the cave and looking in when I got there. I scared it off and carried you out here. I was still thinking of taking you to your mother's cabin, but you seemed to be waking up a bit. You kind of moaned and wrapped your arms around me."

"I don't remember that."

"No? There was even nuzzling."

"Are you pulling my leg?"

"Nope."

"I don't remember that either. I guess I'm glad it was you and not a random Sasquatch that came out of the forest and scooped me up."

"As far as I've seen in my various travels around the world, there's no such thing as Sasquatches."

"I've heard people say there's no such thing as werewolves."

"A valid point. We most certainly exist." Duncan rested his

forehead against mine. "Anyway, because you were stirring, I settled here to wait for you to wake up. Since you seemed to feel amorous, I thought you'd be more inclined to want to get frisky if we were in a romantic forest gully rather than your mom's living room."

A raccoon with glowing red eyes ambled past on the other side of the stream.

"Romantic, huh?" I asked.

"It's a little eerie, but werewolves don't mind things like that."

"You don't think so, huh?"

"No, they find such environments stimulating." Duncan brushed his fingers down the side of my face.

Pleasure swept through me. "I probably hugged on you because of the lingering vestiges of my... I guess you'd say I had a vision."

"One that encouraged you to mate with me? I hope you weren't dreaming of a Sasquatch."

"You *were* featured in the vision." I couldn't quite keep the puzzlement out of my tone as I went on to relay everything to him. It wasn't until I was almost done that it occurred to me to wonder if I should have been so open with him. Somewhere along the way, he'd become a confidant, one who was easy to trust. Maybe that was a mistake, both because of how we'd initially met and because his Lord Abrams—his *creator*—might use his control to learn everything Duncan knew.

"So, my role in your dream was to unearth the wolf case." His tone was dry. "I'm not sure how that led to nuzzling."

"It's possible I was unconsciously pleased with you for lifting me off the cave floor."

"Your foot *was* dangling in the pool."

"I'm lucky it's not glowing red. I should have given you a—" I stopped myself from saying the first thing that came to mind, feeling it would be a little crude at this point in our relationship. Instead, I finished with, "—kiss."

"I'd be amenable to that," he murmured, brushing his lips to my forehead. "Pretty excited by it actually."

My cheeks warmed with the certainty that he knew what I'd almost said. "I figured. You are a guy, after all."

"A guy who's into you."

"Did you hold my boob while I slept?" I smiled up at him, tempted to lift my lips and invite a kiss.

He snorted softly. "I refrained. That would have been presumptuous."

"You did it before while *you* slept."

"A man can't be held responsible for what his body does while he's unconscious."

Since I'd apparently been *nuzzling* him while I'd been knocked out, I didn't tease him further. I merely lifted a hand to his face above mine, brushing my fingers along his strong jaw, the beard stubble bristly against my skin.

"Maybe you should grow this out," I murmured. "So it would be softer and lusher."

"Like my fur when I'm a wolf?"

"Maybe."

"My chin hair is unfortunately a little coarser and not as appealing. I've tried the full-on beard before."

"Hm." I pushed my hand further up the side of his face, threading my fingers into his wavy hair. That was lusher, cool as it fell against my skin, and I kneaded his scalp.

"Luna," Duncan murmured, closing his eyes, longing in his tone.

It pleased me that my touch could make him feel that way, that he was drawn to me for multiple reasons. "Yes?"

With a growl of desire, he lowered his lips to mine. That growl, feral and a little dangerous, tantalized me, making me aware of what he was, a powerful werewolf, not only a playful friend and faithful protector. He was every bit as strong and virile as his teasing jokes promised, and I wanted to be with him.

His kiss was hungry, his body tense underneath me, muscles taut with restraint. I realized he'd probably been thinking of doing this all the while he'd held me and protected me. I wrapped my arms around his shoulders, shifting in his lap for better access to him.

His hand drifted down my throat, stroking my curves through my clothes, and I arched toward him, inviting him to explore. As we kissed, lips brushing, tongues stroking, his fingers slipped under the hem of my shirt and trailed over my bare abdomen. My muscles quivered with delight at his caress, and when he cupped my breast, stroking me through my bra, heat flushed my entire body, heat and desire.

I kissed him harder, nipping at his lip, my fingers curling into his scalp. Need throbbed within me, almost startling in its intensity. By the moon, I hadn't thought I could still be this aroused by a man.

His fingers slid across my abdomen again, trailing lower this time, and I squirmed, almost panting as I pressed up toward him, willing him to unfasten my jeans, to touch more of me.

Another growl drifted from him, sounding far more animal than human. I could feel his hard desire against my body, and he groaned when I shifted, rubbing against him as we kissed and stroked each other. Knowing he was into this excited me. *He* excited me. I stroked him through his shirt, then pushed the fabric upward, wanting to feel his bare body, his hard muscles.

Our lips parted only long enough for the removal of shirts, first his and then mine. As our mouths crashed back together, like the surf meeting the sand, he slid my bra off with practiced ease. He wasn't an inexperienced lover, but I hadn't expected that at his age. As he stroked my breast, sensitive flesh finally bare to him, I felt with certainty that he had the experience to know how to bring me great pleasure. And I wanted that more than I'd wanted anything for a long time.

But something intruded upon my senses, the awareness that we weren't alone. I sensed, at the top of the gully where they could look down upon us, two other werewolves.

My first thought was that we were in danger, that my cousins or some other enemy had found us, but this... This was worse. That was my mother and Rosaria, the wise wolf. I'd forgotten Duncan had said he'd asked my mother to get her.

"Duncan," I murmured, my lips pressed against his.

It was hard to pull away, to stop. My fingers kept running over his shoulders and the back of his head, rubbing and kneading. I longed to give in to passion, to let Duncan take me.

He hadn't yet stopped stroking and kissing me. With his greater senses, he had to know witnesses were up there. Did he not care? Or maybe he was so distracted that he *didn't* know we had an audience.

"I think she's okay," came distant amused words. Rosaria.

"Apparently so," my mother said. "I hope he gets her with child."

I groaned, not, this time, because of arousal. Duncan stiffened, also not because of arousal, and turned his head to look toward them.

Silver light bathed his face, and only then did I realize that the medallion still around my neck had started glowing. Above me, Duncan was breathing as heavily as I, and sweat dampened his skin. He was beautiful and magnificent and... his face was hard when he looked toward our observers. Observers who, thanks to the magical light, could see everything we were doing as if a roadside flare had been set up on my chest. I groaned again.

Rosaria and my mother must have noticed us looking at them. They backed away, but their voices continued to float down.

"I want grandchildren," my mom said.

"You *have* grandchildren," Rosaria reminded her.

"Not from her loins. She's the only one who came from him, from the one who stirred my passions like none other, and who had the power of the ancients." She wasn't talking about Lorenzo but my long-gone father.

Duncan shifted away, and disappointment swept through me. I was tempted to sit up and try to reclaim the moment, but I didn't want him to think there was any truth to my mom's words, that I'd kissed him because I wanted him to give me *offspring*. The moon forbid, I had no desire to have babies again. I didn't care what my mother wanted.

"I'm sorry." My ears and sense for the magical told me that Mom and Rosaria had left the area, heading back to the cabin and giving us privacy now that they'd made sure I didn't need help, but the moment had passed. "I don't want you because of, you know." I waved vaguely toward my uterus.

"I know," Duncan said, but there was a distance to him now.

Mom had definitely ruined the moment.

"I didn't even *want* you up until recently."

He managed a faint smile. "I know that too. You're still ambivalent about me."

"I don't think my kiss was that ambivalent," I muttered, wondering if I'd left fingernail marks on his shoulders.

"No." His smile broadened. "I enjoyed it. I..." He squinted, peering toward the top of the gully.

I couldn't detect any werewolves up there, but that didn't mean Mom wasn't headed back.

"Did you intend to confront your cousins tonight?" Duncan asked quietly.

"I intended to ask my mom if she was *okay* with me confronting them. If I can't convince the elders to do anything."

Duncan nodded, his gaze still toward the top of the gully. "And?"

"You were there. I almost think she wants me to challenge them, but she also said that if I could get evidence of their wrong-doing, the elders might kick them out of their own accord."

Duncan rose to his feet, grabbed our shirts, and gave me mine while offering a hand up. "It's good that she didn't forbid you to fight them."

"Why?" I accepted his hand warily, letting him pull me to my feet. "They're not here, are they?"

"They are. Augustus and several others."

"Hell."

13

AGAIN FULLY CLOTHED, DUNCAN AND I WALKED OUT OF THE GULLY and toward the cabin. Once we climbed out of the depression, I could also sense other werewolves in the area. Mom was in the cabin, and the others were lurking in her driveway.

"It's after midnight." I'd glanced at my phone as we'd climbed. "You'd think they would have elsewhere to be."

"Someone may have told them you were here." Duncan slanted me a look.

Was he implying the pack *wise wolf* would have gotten involved? I was sure my mom hadn't reached out to my cousins. She might accept it was the way of the wolf if I confronted them and died, but... she wanted me to live and be her heir. At that very moment, I wore the medallion she intended to leave to me. She wouldn't have told them I was here tonight.

It must have been Rosaria. Or maybe chance had brought my cousins by—this did seem to be a favorite launching point for wolves heading out to hunt. I also thought of the magical driveway devices we'd passed and wondered again who had set them up for

Mom. Was it possible they reported whenever someone came onto the property? Like magical security cameras?

A howl came from the driveway, raising the hair on the back of my neck. That was one of my cousins, one who'd helped Augustus attack me on the train trestle the night of the hunt.

At the cabin, two more trucks had joined mine in the parking area. No, not *joined*. They were hemming mine in. Trapping it.

I swallowed and told myself I could drive off road and escape if needed. There weren't so many trees lining the driveway that I couldn't find a route out. But I didn't want to escape. I wanted evidence, or, even better, a confession. Ideally one that Mom would hear. Mom and Lorenzo. Was he around? No, I sensed five or six male werewolves in the driveway, but I didn't detect his aura.

When we stopped out front, we found Mom on the porch of her cabin, the wise wolf still with her. These were enough witnesses, surely. If Mom and Rosaria told Lorenzo to kick Augustus and his trouble-making siblings out of the pack, Lorenzo would gather enough elders and less wayward young wolves to make it happen. I was certain of it.

Augustus, Marco, and two more of my cousins waited about fifteen yards up the driveway from the cabin. They were in human form, standing to further block the way out. Two more of their allies who were shape-changed into wolves lurked in the trees.

All eyes were turned toward me. Me and Duncan.

He walked calmly at my side. Augustus sneered when their eyes met.

"Don't you go anywhere without that scruffy loner?" Marco asked me.

"No. I like him." I stopped near my truck, not getting too close to my cousins.

Augustus's sleeves were rolled up to show off his muscled fore-arms. He looked like he had come to fight. With Duncan's help, I'd defeated my cousins before, badly enough that they would be fools to attack while he was here with me. But Augustus might have more than muscles up his sleeves.

"Do you think you can change again tonight if we need to?" I asked Duncan quietly.

"Easily."

The medallion had stopped glowing, but Augustus noticed it around my neck. His sneer shifted to a scowl.

"Presumptuous of you to wear that. Did you ask permission?" He looked toward the porch.

"I asked her to take it to the sacred cave," Mom said calmly.

She said *the sacred cave* like she expected Augustus to know all about the place. Maybe it wasn't the secret I'd believed. Abruptly, I realized that Augustus might have known about it and its magic for a long time. Maybe, as I'd been thinking earlier, he *had* taken water from that pool to feed the pack of wolves and mongrel dogs that he'd sent at me. That could have accounted for their glowing eyes.

"What brings you here tonight, Augustus?" Mom asked. "Lorenzo and I told you not to bother Luna further."

Augustus raised his chin. "She has been badmouthing me and besmirching my honor."

I snorted. "What honor? You're a toad."

Augustus pointed at me. "Like that. She has spoken this way to outsiders, to others with power."

"If you mean I've told others that you tried to kill me, I didn't think that was a secret." I actually couldn't think of many people I'd complained to about Augustus. Since I hardly told anyone I was a werewolf, I couldn't admit that I had annoying lupine cousins. "And what honor did I besmirch?" I glanced at Mom and Rosaria. "You're the one making a bad name for the pack by acting like the mafia."

I willed Augustus to reply in such a way that would verify that.

"I don't know what you're talking about," Augustus said, "but you've been telling anyone who will listen that I'm not fit to lead the pack."

I was *positive* I hadn't brought that up to anyone.

His eyes narrowed. "I intend to prove myself fit. To redeem my honor in the eyes of my relatives, I challenge you to a battle. *One-on-one*." He glared at Duncan as he said that last.

I opened my mouth, tempted to accept the challenge without thought—since the last dose of the werewolf sublimation had long since worn off, I believed I could best him. But he had to have treachery in mind. After I'd knocked him off the train trestle, he couldn't be certain he could best me in a fair fight. What was he up to?

"You hesitate, Luna?" Augustus asked softly. "It's possible you're not an appropriate heir for that medallion."

"It's possible you're an asshole."

"*I* didn't turn my back on my heritage and abandon my people and my own *mother* for more than twenty years."

"She probably wishes you had," I grumbled before I could catch myself. He was bringing me down to his schoolyard-bully level, and I didn't want that. Not in front of Mom or Duncan—or myself, for that matter. "I haven't besmirched your honor or spoken of you at all, but I'm not afraid to fight you one-on-one if you need to prove something. Though I don't think you'll find a battle against me will come out in your favor."

"We shall see." Augustus took a few steps back and pointed to the open driveway behind him. "Come and face me. If you're not afraid."

"He's up to something," Duncan said.

"Oh I know."

Augustus removed his shirt and tossed it onto one of the trucks. "Are you game, Luna? Let us settle this like wolves."

His challenging words and stare made me want to roll my eyes and walk away, but my wolf blood felt differently. Detecting the threat, my instincts summoned my magic, and my skin pricked, flushing with warmth, with the promise of a change.

Whether Duncan sensed the call coming to me or not, I didn't know, but he looked over. "If you accept, I'll make sure the others don't interfere."

"There are a lot of them."

"There's a lot of *me*." His smile was almost savage. He *wanted* to fight them.

"I'm willing to take him on, but what I really want is to get him to confess in front of witnesses." I nodded toward the porch.

"Confess to being an obnoxious ass who challenges females?" Duncan asked.

"To being an obnoxious ass who, in the name of the pack, extorts business owners when he's not busy skulking about, waiting for opportunities to steal invaluable artifacts." I glanced toward my truck, reminded that the case was in the glove box. By habit, I'd locked the vehicle, but I wondered if my cousins had sensed the artifact in there.

"He might not admit to that unless you're standing on his throat."

"He would look good with a paw crushing his Adam's apple," I said.

"Agreed."

I bumped elbows with Duncan before walking forward by myself, my skin hot with the magic of the impending change. If I didn't remove my clothes soon, I risked losing them, but Augustus couldn't confess once he changed into a wolf.

"I'll only fight you on your terms," I said, "if you tell us all why you're extorting business owners who have paranormal blood and doing it in the name of the pack. Not only in Snohomish County but in King County too. Why do you need money? You're a wolf and hunt for your food."

"I don't know what you're talking about," Augustus said again.

I folded my arms over my chest. "Then I'm not fighting you."

"That would make you a coward and not worthy to inherit anything from your mother." Eyes challenging, Augustus looked toward the porch.

Mom didn't say anything. After our conversation, I knew she believed my cousins were obnoxious pains in the asses, but I also knew she wouldn't stop a formal challenge from playing out in her driveway. She would also think less of me if I didn't accept it.

"If I were stupid enough to fall for whatever scheme you've cooked up, *then* I wouldn't be worthy," I said. "The bartender of El Gato Mágico knows who you are and can identify you. If you're going to be a brutish thug, maybe you should use another name."

A hint of uncertainty flashed in Augustus's eyes, but he masked it by bending to remove his shoes. I hoped my mom had caught that look, that she believed what I'd told her.

"Also," I added, "maybe you should *actually* stop crime in the area if you're going to charge people for doing so."

"Maybe you should start taking off your clothes and change so we can get this over with." Augustus tossed his shoes and socks aside.

Behind me, Duncan removed his shirt.

Augustus had started to reach for his fly, but he paused. "This duel doesn't involve you, loner."

"I'm here to ensure the duel remains fair and under the conditions you proposed," Duncan said coolly. "One-on-one."

"And here I thought he was here to screw her," Marco muttered, drawing laughs from the others.

Duncan turned his cold gaze on them. For a guy who was smiling and affable most of the time, he could do menacing well when he wanted. Maybe it was because we were all magical and could sense the feral power that emanated from him.

Marco and the others shifted to the side of the driveway,

leaving Augustus standing alone. They didn't go far though; they remained close enough that they could leap in at any time.

Duncan tossed his shirt over the railing of the porch. I took a deep breath, reassured that he could also jump in at any time.

"If I beat you, I want your word that you'll leave the business owners alone," I said.

"I still have no idea *what* you're talking about, coz." Augustus waved a dismissive hand, then removed his jeans. "We're dueling tonight because you've besmirched my honor."

"Do you even know what that word means?"

"I know a lot." Now naked in the driveway, Augustus held my gaze. "And I know you're not worthy to be welcomed back into the pack. You left us. You don't have any right to be here now."

I bristled, skin flushing even hotter. Part of it was magic, the call of the wolf, and part of it was anger. Anger and... shame. Even if I'd had a reason for leaving, I couldn't help but feel that he was right on some level. I shouldn't have abandoned my family, my mother.

"Wolves leave, and they come back," was what I said. "If they've the power to earn a place in the pack, they deserve one."

"Let's see if you do." Augustus beckoned with his fingers, then took a few more steps back and dropped to all fours, the change coming over him.

Frustrated that he hadn't given a confession—if anything, he was doing his best to make me look petty in front of Mom and Rosaria—I felt the magic surging up within me, demanding to be released. Though I worried I was walking into a trap, I removed the medallion and my clothes. Duncan had my back, and I... I realized I trusted him. Even if our relationship had started with betrayal, I believed wholeheartedly that he would help me against my family. He would be here for me if I needed him.

And I probably would. As the magic transformed me, my last human thought was that I was most certainly walking into a trap.

But the need to prove myself, to not back down in front of my mother or be perceived as a coward by the pack, drove me.

Skin stretching, torso changing, and fur sprouting, I dropped to all fours, paws feeling the compact dirt of the driveway. The magic prompted me to lift my head and howl.

Behind me, my ally remained in his human form, but he'd also removed his clothes. He could change quickly when the need arose.

The dark-gray wolf that was Augustus had backed farther down the driveway, making sure nobody was nearby as he waited, cold eyes intent. I padded toward him with determination.

It crossed my mind that he was pulling me farther from the cabin, from Mom's witnessing eyes. But she wouldn't stop this. She'd made it clear by not interfering thus far. As a devotee to the way of the wolf, she would stand back and watch Augustus kill me, if he could. In her eyes, if I couldn't fend him off, I didn't deserve to live.

As I drew closer, I sensed magic in the woods on either side of the driveway. I hesitated with confusion until a vague memory from my other form eased through my mind. The magical security devices to deter enemies of the pack. They'd been there before. Mom had ordered them installed. My cousins shouldn't have had anything to do with them.

But as I padded closer, drawing even with the first of several devices in the ferns, and the dark-gray wolf's jaws parted with smugness and triumph, I realized that might not be true. Augustus might have backed down the driveway, not because of Mom's eyes or to give us more room, but to lure me closer to the devices.

I halted. My cousin had started this. Let him come to me.

Augustus took a few more steps backward before accepting that I wouldn't follow him farther. He looked intently toward one of his observing siblings. Orazio. Did he have something in his hand?

While I was trying to figure that out, Augustus charged.

I settled my weight, bracing myself, my gaze locked on his throat. His jaws parted as he sprang for me.

It crossed my mind to dodge, but he might expect that. Instead, I surged straight into him, using my snout to knock his aside as our chests crashed together. His weight was jarring, and fangs brushed my face, but I managed to deflect most of the bite. With his head pushed aside, I snapped for his throat. He tried to jerk his snout down to cover the vulnerable spot, but I got there first, fangs sinking into fur and flesh.

He pushed with his legs, trying to shove me back. If we'd been human, it would have worked, but we were close to the same size as wolves. I bunched my muscles and resisted as I dug my fangs in deeper. He snapped his own jaws, but with mine locked around his throat, he couldn't find the angle to sink his teeth into me.

He tried rearing up on his hind legs, but I wouldn't let him go. With the taste of his blood in my mouth, my savage instincts were taking over, demanding that I hold fast until my enemy died. But I needed a better angle to turn my grip into a death bite. When I loosened my jaws slightly to reposition, he dropped to his belly and rolled to the side. I almost caught him again before he could get away, but he whipped himself off the driveway and into the ferns.

I started after him, but the magical devices remained in my senses. I hadn't forgotten them.

Neck bleeding, Augustus rose to all fours. He snarled at me from the brush, then turned his head, showing his neck. Trying to taunt me to jump in after him. There was a device behind him, and I had no idea what it did.

I backed a few steps toward the cabin and flicked an ear, taunting *him*.

Coward, I thought, though we had no way to communicate telepathically. With body language, I showed him my feelings.

He was the one to be lured closer, to run toward me. This time, I dodged, though I was careful to stay on the driveway. I didn't *know* if it was a safe haven, but I wouldn't risk getting close to the devices.

He snapped at me, but I was too fast and evaded him. He rushed past; then, as he stopped himself to turn, I whirled toward him. Jaws leading, I snapped for his flank. This time, I landed a series of fast bites instead of holding on. If I latched onto his back half for long, he would have space to maneuver, time to twist and sink his jaws into me.

When he tried that, I released my last bite and jumped back. The scent of his blood filled the air as it spattered onto the dirt driveway.

Panting, he faced me again. But he paused to glance toward our observers, toward Orazio, still in his human form. He nodded right before Augustus charged at me again.

Prepared, I was about to dodge, but purple beams shot out from the ferns on either side of the driveway. The magic slammed into me hard enough to knock me flying as pain scorched my torso.

I managed to evade Augustus's jaws as he ran in, but my dodge turned into a clumsy tumble. I rolled off the driveway and into a tree.

The beams followed me, continuing to burn pain into me. Not giving me any reprieve, Augustus leaped after me to take advantage. Despite the pain, I met his jaws with mine, snapping with fury for his face, longing to gouge out his eyes and drive my fangs through his skull.

In his haste to take advantage and bring me down, he let one of the beams clip his shoulder. He cried out like he'd been electrocuted. Still enduring the pain, I lunged for his throat.

I would have gotten him, a clean and killing bite, but another wolf charged in from the side and knocked me flying. The one-on-one fight had ended.

14

As I leaped to my feet, pummeled by lupine enemies as well as magical beams that tracked me no matter where I went, a great roar came from further up the driveway.

That was Duncan. Duncan as the bipedfuris?

Through the trees and ferns, I couldn't spot him. All I could see were wolves trying to surround me and end my life.

I snapped left and right to keep them back and put my rump against a tree so they couldn't come in from behind. Only the need to avoid the beams themselves kept my cousins from charging me as one unit and getting through my defenses.

Only that and Duncan. In his powerful two-legged form, he sprang into the fray, not caring a whit about the beams.

He picked up one of the wolves with his clawed hands, hefted him over his head, and hurled our enemy across the driveway and at a tree. No, *into* a tree. I gaped as one of my cousins ended up dangling in the branches ten feet up.

The dark-gray wolf that was Augustus glanced at Duncan with shock and fear in his eyes. That didn't keep Augustus from lunging for me once more, determined to take me out before he lost the support of his allies.

Having no trouble reading his intent, I saw the attack coming. When he charged toward my head, I dropped low and lunged at him. My jaws clamped around his forelimb, crunching into bone.

He yelped and tried to pull away. I would have ground his bone to dust, but his gyrations pulled my head toward one of the beams. With purple flashing in my eyes, I released Augustus and dropped low. The beam skimmed past, searing my ear.

Another thud and yelp sounded, Duncan hurling another foe away. After that, he charged at one of the men—Orazio.

I rolled to my feet, ready for my cousin to attack again, but the beams vanished. Augustus glanced about, as if startled and betrayed by their disappearance.

I snarled, ready to charge him. He looked at me, at Duncan, and then backed away.

The yell of a man came next—a cry from Orazio. Something crunched. The magical controller he'd been holding. I sensed the power of the devices all around me diminishing.

I stepped into the driveway, expecting another attack, but my foes were backing away. With Orazio and the beams dealt with, Duncan sprang close, startling me. Fear swept through me as I remembered that he'd turned into an enemy at the potion factory. But he landed beside me, not in front of me, and he threw his head back and roared.

A tingle of foreign magic turned the air electric around us and made my hackles rise. Was it another security device that would strike us?

Duncan paused, head cocked, as if listening.

I snarled a warning, spotting another of my cousins in human form. Standing to the side of the driveway, he had a rifle in his hand, the weapon pointed at us. He wavered back and forth with his aim, as if he couldn't decide if he should shoot Duncan or me.

Fury filled me. This had gone far beyond a duel, one-on-one or otherwise. Augustus had spoken of honor, but these bastards had none.

My armed cousin settled on Duncan, aiming at his muscled torso. Fueled by contempt and fury, I charged into the brush, running so fast that it surprised my cousin. His finger jerked as he pulled the trigger, and the bullet went wide. It left a silver streak in the air before it thudded into a distant tree.

I'd seen those bullets before. In the hands of enemies of the pack. How had my cousin gotten such projectiles?

Hardly caring, I sank my teeth into his thigh, biting deep. He screamed and slammed the rifle into my back.

Shrugging off the blow, I released my bite to whip my head around and catch the barrel of the weapon. The cold metal tasted foul in my mouth. I crunched down, tore it from his grip, and flung it into the woods.

My cousin cursed and crouched, arms spread, fingers curled. He appeared to be on the verge of shifting into wolf form, but he grabbed his wounded thigh and glanced at the driveway. Duncan hadn't moved, but he roared again, arms spread and muscles taut, making him look impressive. And dangerous. But his furred face contorted, as if he battled an inner demon. Or a magical call?

My cousin looked at me. What he saw on my face, I didn't know, but he didn't shift forms, not with me so close that I could have taken advantage during the seconds he would be vulnerable. I could have killed him.

He turned and ran, limping heavily on his wounded leg.

When I looked around for more foes, I was surprised to find Duncan, still in the bipedfuris form, running down the driveway toward the road. There was no enemy chasing him, and he didn't tear off at top speed out of fear. He loped away, as if called to start a journey.

Duncan looked back, his eyes aggrieved when they met mine,

but he didn't slow down. He turned onto the road and headed north.

For reasons that didn't fully register to my wolf brain, he was leaving me alone.

Fortunately, further enemies did not present themselves. Augustus and the others were slinking off into the woods.

Seething, I was tempted to go after him, the savagery in my blood wanting to continue the battle, to utterly defeat he who'd challenged me. He who'd challenged me ignobly and cheated instead of allowing a fair fight.

But my ally—the only ally around who'd jumped in to help— had disappeared, summoned by magic that superseded the power of the wolf. The memory of the magic I'd noticed a minute before lingered, though I could no longer sense it. Soon, I could no longer sense the bipedfuris either.

Reluctantly, I let my cousins leave without giving chase. If I went after them and they realized I was alone, they would turn on me again. I might yet know defeat this night.

As I stood in the driveway, thoughts whirling, the wolf magic faded. I sank back onto my haunches as the change came. When I was once again in my human form, the night air cold against my bare skin, I rose and walked toward the cabin.

Blood dripped from the fang wounds in my shoulder, and the beams had left burn marks on my sides. The injuries throbbed as I walked. I hoped the bite, in particular, would heal quickly. That was the arm I used to clean apartments.

Rosaria had disappeared, but my mother remained on the porch.

Annoyed, I clenched my jaw as I gathered my clothes and picked up Duncan's as well. Since Mom was old and ill, I wouldn't have expected her to help in a fight, but she could have done *something* when she'd witnessed the treachery. Yelled at my cousins to knock it off anyway. Or called Lorenzo or someone else to break up the fight—or turn off those damn magical devices.

But she'd only watched. Waiting to see if I passed the test? Something told me that was it. She'd spoken of the arbiter and driving Augustus out of the pack if he deserved it, but she wanted me to handle my problems on my own.

"Thanks for the help," I couldn't keep from saying sarcastically.

"What would you wish me to have done? The victory was yours to earn. If you seek to have a place of respect in the pack again, you should defeat him. It is what would convince others that you have the right to be here. And it is what you need, as well, to be sure of yourself and whether you deserve a place in the pack after your long absence."

"I'm forty-five, Mom. I don't need a damn coming-of-age test."

She looked off into the woods in the direction Duncan had gone. "He can become the bipedfuris."

Was that... reverence in her tone?

"That is what I sensed all along," she mused. "I didn't quite realize it. I've not encountered another werewolf with the power to become a two-legs, not in my entire life." She cocked her head. "What called him away?"

"It's a long story."

She looked at me. "You knew he could change into that form?"

"I haven't known for long, but yes."

"He would be an even more suitable mate. Perhaps your offspring would also have that ability."

I stared at her. I was naked, tired, and battered, with blood running down my arm, and all she cared about was my offspring?

Maybe she guessed my thoughts. "Do you want me to call back Rosaria?"

"To opine on Duncan's suitability as a mate?"

"She got the gist of that when we came across you in the woods."

My cheeks heated, and I glowered at her. Because they'd *come across* us in the woods, Duncan and I hadn't done anything to indicate suitability or anything else.

"To tend your wound," Mom said, waving at my shoulder. "Come inside, if you like. I'll get you something to drink and eat if you're hungry."

"I'm fine." I laid the medallion on the porch railing for her. "I'll wait in my truck for Duncan to come back."

She raised her eyebrows. "I have dark chocolate with crunchy cacao nibs."

That was the kind I'd given to the werewolf boy—to Duncan's clone brother. I wondered if the kid had liked it or had been disappointed it wasn't sweeter. I also wondered if Duncan would see his clone again tonight. The potion factory was the only place I could imagine him being called to.

"I've got my own." I waved a curt goodnight and walked stiffly to my truck.

Maybe Mom had intended the chocolate as a peace offering, but I was still too disgruntled to accept it.

"You fought well, my daughter," she called softly after me. "Were he not a deceitful coyote instead of a true wolf, you would have won."

"Damn straight." I tried to unknot my shoulders and set aside my dour mood.

"I worry for Lorenzo when Augustus decides to make his move and turns that deceit on him." Her words were soft, more for herself and the night than for me. "I worry for the future of the pack unless something changes."

Unless I did something? The weight of the family's future settled on my shoulders, more burdensome than the bite wound.

15

It was dawn by the time I pulled into the parking lot at Sylvan Serenity. Gigantic yawns kept making my eyes water, but I couldn't decide if I wanted to stumble into bed or pull multiple shots of liquid caffeine from my espresso maker. Since it was Monday and a regular workday, the tenants would need me. Too bad I'd gotten home so late—so early.

After the fight, I'd waited two hours in my truck, expecting Duncan to return, but he never did. That had left me worried for him—and glad I'd been the one to drive up to Mom's house. I hoped he could find his own way home.

Home? I snorted as I got out of the truck. This was my home, not his. What he considered the parking lot where he'd parked his van, I didn't know. The equivalent of a hotel, I supposed.

His words about having been lonely growing up came to mind. Maybe *more* than growing up. With all his traveling, he probably had acquaintances all over the world, but had he ever had a home?

As I headed along the walkway toward my apartment, I smiled in some bemusement at the complex. Strange that it was more of a

home to me than anyplace else, but after twenty years and raising
my boys here, it probably wasn't surprising.

I stutter-stepped when I remembered the Sylvans' visit. And
the possibility that they might sell the property.

I needed to find a way to resolve things with my cousins and
ensure no more crime or trouble of any kind touched the complex.
I didn't want the Sylvans to have any more reasons to sell. Hopefully, it wasn't already too late.

A wolf lying on her belly at my front door and daintily eating a
rabbit made me stutter-step again. She also drove the thoughts of
losing my home out of my mind for the moment.

The wolf looked at me, her aura and bright green eyes familiar.
She was black with two white paws and a white-tipped tail, which
she wagged at me as she rose to all fours.

"I'm definitely not installing doorbell cams," I muttered.

The wolf tilted her head curiously. This clearly wasn't one of
Augustus's surly allies. As I walked closer, I recognized her.

"Oh, hi, Jasmine." I had only seen her as a wolf once before,
when I'd recently hunted with the pack, and there had been a *lot*
of wolves around that night.

She swished her tail again and gulped down the rest of the
rabbit, leaving a few blood spatters and tufts of fur on the cement.

"That's okay. I need to pressure wash the walkways this winter
anyway." I looked around, hoping nobody was outside, watching
me chat up a wolf.

Her meal complete, Jasmine padded into a rhododendron, one
of the few shrubs on the property that didn't lose its leaves in the
winter. This one was large enough to completely hide a wolf,
though when the leaves started rustling, I raised my eyebrows.

"I hope you're not doing something I'll feel compelled to bag
up later." I waved toward the dog-waste station I'd had Duncan
refill the day before, though I suspected Jasmine was changing.

A moment later, her human head stuck up from the center of

the rhododendron, her black hair mussed around her face. She stuck her tongue out at me as she hunched to keep her bare shoulders low. She looked like she was fastening a bra, one with a few twigs sticking out of it.

"I've been waiting for you *forever*. I got bored and went to hunt, but there's nothing good around here." Jasmine wrinkled her nose in the direction of the tufts of fur.

"Surprisingly few herds of deer nosh on our lawn. I don't think they're fans of freeway noise and densely packed suburban areas."

With all the new apartments going up, Shoreline might well qualify as *urban* by now.

"Deer are all over the place by our house in Redmond." Jasmine shifted and grunted as she remained in the rhododendron, tugging up a pair of jeans.

"There's still some acreage out there and places where the homes are farther apart. And you're not that far from larger wooded areas and farmlands."

"The deer like the grass and bushes that people plant around their houses. They're half tame, so we don't usually hunt them. Dad says it isn't fair, that they're dumbed down, just like humans who never had to build their own computers or install operating systems with floppy disks." She rolled her eyes at the analogy.

"How is your software-developer father?" I wondered if he'd done any more research into the relics or Radomir's corporation that had factories and farms all around Puget Sound, apparently raking in the dough since perfumes and potions were a high-margin business. I didn't yet know how profitable stealing wolf artifacts was.

"He's fine. But that's not what I came to talk to you about. I—" Jasmine looked toward the walkway a second before Bolin stepped around the corner of the building, his short hair tousled, two coffee drinks in his hands, and bags under his eyes.

Only half-dressed, Jasmine slunk low in the rhododendron,

though it wasn't tall enough to completely hide her, not when she was in human form. She did, however, manage to find camouflage for *most* of her body.

"Hi, Bolin." I almost added that he was here early, especially given his loathing for morning hours, but with a glance at my phone telling me it was eight a.m, I was again reminded of the approach of the winter solstice. Dawn was not at an impressively early hour.

"Hi."

The rhododendron shivered, and he started to look toward it.

"Is one of those for me?" I asked to distract him, not because I expected him to share. Besides, my own espresso maker lay scant feet away inside my apartment.

Bolin curled the cups protectively to his chest. "No." He looked me over, his gaze lingering on my hair, and loosened his grip on one. "Did you spend the night in the woods again?"

"Yeah. The allure of lumpy cave floors and beds of ferns can't be resisted." I thought wistfully about the allure of Duncan's strong arms around me, gently *cuddling* me, as he'd put it. It had been nice. If only my *mom* hadn't shown up...

"Is there something wrong with your bed here?" Bolin nodded toward my apartment door.

"There aren't enough fir needles and fern fronds embedded in the mattress for comfort."

A giggle came from the rhododendron.

Bolin blinked in surprise and looked at it. "I thought that was Duncan in there."

"No. He does not, as far as I've ever seen, feel compelled to hide his nudity behind leaves, clothes, or any other sight-blocking items." I thought of my blanket and wondered if it was still in his van.

"Oh, I've noticed." Bolin hesitated, then offered me the coffee cup with a plain lid. He never gave up the drink with whipped

I refrained from pointing out that the birds might, in fact, be smart enough to recognize the lack of predatory capability in a plastic raptor.

"Anyway," Bolin said, "I came to tell you that the Donovans in C-4 moved out yesterday and turned their key in to the dropbox instead of showing up in person for their checkout today. Once I went by the apartment, I could see why. I can't believe people live like that. They left garbage all over the floors, beer cans on every surface, cat poop in the bathroom, urine-stained mattresses leaning against the wall, a couch with the cushions removed, and moldy and unidentifiable food in the refrigerator. *And* they stole the switch plates. *All* of them. Luna, switch plates aren't worth anything, are they? I've heard of copper wiring in walls having some modest financial value, but..."

"No. Switch plates don't cost much to replace at least." In my twenty-odd years as a property manager, I'd seen it all, so the description didn't faze me.

"Why would you *take* them?"

I spread my arms. "Why would you let your cat poop on the floor?"

"I don't know, but the whole place stinks. I almost passed out when I went in."

"Ah. For future reference, there's an M-50 military-grade gas mask in the leasing office."

He scrutinized me. "I... kind of think you're not joking."

"Nope. Are you enjoying your internship?" I grinned at him.

"I..." He trailed off, his gaze drawn to the rhododendron again.

Jasmine, clothed now except for socks and sneakers that she carried in her hand, had left the leaf cover and was walking toward us. She must not have wanted to try to put them on while standing on the damp earth. A lot of dew smothered the grass this morning.

"It's, uhm, interesting." Bolin's wide-eyed gaze locked on her.

"Yup. This is my niece, Jasmine. Jasmine, this is Bolin. He works here."

Bolin gave me an aggrieved look, at which point I realized his wide eyes might have less to do with surprise than interest.

"Temporarily," I added. "He's getting real-world work experience before heading off as a well-paid, world-traveling accountant who'll have a share in his family's lucrative apartment business."

Bolin straightened with pride at this more flattering description, though maybe I should have talked up his personal traits instead of mentioning his parents' money. Not that most werewolves cared about such things.

"Huh." Jasmine waved absently at Bolin, then fished a leaf out of her hair and sat down on the dry walkway to put on her socks and shoes. "Aunt Luna, I came because I need to talk to you about something."

"Do you have enlightening news on the artifacts?"

"No."

"I was afraid of that." I fished out my keys to unlock my door.

"I assume you don't want me to return the Donovans' damage deposit?" Bolin glanced at me while gazing wistfully at Jasmine, who was brushing dirt off her bare soles before tugging on her socks.

"No. The turn will cost us a lot more than they put down. I'm sure they'll call and pretend to be mystified about *why* they aren't getting it back though." I wasn't that sure about that. Since they'd dropped off the key and slunk away in the night, they probably knew they were disgusting slobs.

"I figured. I can deal with them if they try to get aggressive." Bolin stood straight, though it was hard for someone to look tough with mussed hair, bags under the eyes, and coffee cups clutched like security blankets.

"Good," I said.

Busy tying her shoes, Jasmine didn't look at him. I had a feeling she was unaware that he thought she was cute and wasn't intentionally giving him the cold shoulder.

"Do you have a cleaning service you use that you want me to call?" Bolin asked. "Or do you handle everything yourself?"

"You've seen me scouring the toxic clingy residue out of a unit that was occupied by a smoker. Do you really need to ask?"

"I wasn't sure if cat poop would prompt you to outsource this one."

"Nope. I might wear the mask though." I winked at him as I opened my door.

"There's also mold on the nasty shower curtain and ceiling in the bathroom," he warned. "I'll wager the Donovans never once turned on the fan."

"Probably not. Did they take the switch plate for that too?"

"No, they left the fan controls alone. They did take the one for the light."

"People are interesting."

"That's one word for it."

"I'll let you know when I've got everything cleaned," I said, "and then you can help me apply some of the special mold-inhibitor paint you made."

It was a potion, not paint, but he hid his druidic talents since his mother had forbidden him from studying the ancient arts, so I knew he would prefer I not mention them in front of a witness. Even if Jasmine would be unfazed by the existence of druids.

"Okay," he said.

By now, Jasmine had finished dressing and stood. She caught my gaze and tilted her head meaningfully toward the open door.

"Anything else, Bolin?" I asked.

"Not that I can't handle."

"Great. Thanks." I thumped him on the shoulder.

As my niece started through the door, he said, "It was nice meeting you, Jasmine."

She looked distracted, probably by the news she intended to give me, but managed a smile and a wave for him. "Sure. You too, uhm, Bolin, right?"

"Yes." Never had someone beamed such pleasure because a woman remembered his name. "Here." He thrust a coffee cup toward her, the one with whipped cream on top. Goodness. "I just got it a few minutes ago and haven't taken a drink."

"Oh." Jasmine brightened with interest and reached for it before pausing to look at me.

Asking if there would be strings attached? I wasn't sure, but I nodded, sure Bolin wouldn't be too much of a pest. He seemed to accept *no* from women without more than disappointment.

"Cool, thanks." Jasmine accepted the cup, waved again, and turned on the lights as she stepped inside.

Between the late sunrise and gray sky, not much natural daylight permeated my apartment this time of year.

"Sorry I was gone all night," I said after closing the door. "I was up at Mom's."

"I *thought* you might have gone up there. But I wasn't sure. You could have gone somewhere with your hot guy too."

"Technically, I did." I cast a worried look toward a north-facing window, thoughts of Duncan's disappearance returning to mind.

"Oh! Did you get horizontal?" Jasmine sipped from the coffee, made a contented sound, and cradled it to her chest.

"Not for long. Not with Mom in the area."

Jasmine wrinkled her nose. "That would be a deterrent. Aunt Umbra is even sterner than my mom. She probably doesn't like Duncan because he's a lone wolf and didn't bring an offering when he showed up in the area."

"She's okay with him now." I did not mention Mom's words on mating with him and birthing babies. "I also had a showdown with Augustus when I was there."

"That's what I came to warn you about. He's gunning for you."

"He tricked me into dueling him one-on-one last night, but he got treacherous and didn't play fair. If you can imagine." I briefly summarized the fight for her, leaving out the part where Duncan had turned into a bipedfuris. She would hear about it eventually, but I felt compelled to keep his secrets. Or at least not be the one to blab them.

"Shoot, I'd hoped to warn you about that *before* you ran into

Augustus again. He called a family meeting last night, but it was out at his lake house in Sammamish, not in the traditional spot, the hunting grounds by your mom's cabin."

"His lake house?" I asked, though I'd heard about the home already. "You say that like he's got *multiple* houses. He's not scamming enough money out of people for *that,* is he?"

Sammamish, home to hordes of highly paid IT people that overflowed from Redmond and Bellevue, was an expensive suburb in which to live. Even if Augustus had the money for it, however ill-gotten, it was hard for me to imagine my thugly cousin fitting in there. Jasmine's dad, maybe. I'd yet to meet him, but he sounded like a hardcore geek.

Jasmine shrugged. "I heard there's a home in Arizona too."

"*Arizona*? It's *hot* there for someone furry."

"For anyone without scales, I'd think. The snakes reputedly sunbathe when the temperatures rise over a hundred."

"I'd say Augustus isn't a snake, but that's not really true."

Jasmine snorted. "I think the home is in Sedona. There's some elevation there, so it's not as hot and snake-laden. It's pretty though, in a scorched-earth, red-rocks kind of way."

"I'll take your word for it." My salary had never been such that vacations to exotic places had been affordable. "Did you go to the meeting? Or did someone blab about what Augustus said?"

"I *did* go." Jasmine's eyes gleamed as she sipped the coffee. "To be a mole."

"Better than a snake, I suppose."

"A mole as in a *spy* that is cleverly inserted into the enemy camp. To get hot intel for you."

I hesitated, not sure if I should encourage such activity or worry that Augustus would find out Jasmine was relaying presumably secret information to me.

"I'm honored that you would want to do that, but... it's a little dangerous for you, isn't it? Augustus doesn't seem to be above hurting family members." Hell, he'd been trying to *kill* me.

"He doesn't know I'm not loyal and happy to follow along with his schemes to overthrow Lorenzo and get rid of anyone who opposes him." Jasmine pointed the coffee cup at me.

"I didn't oppose him until he started trying to kill me. He brought that on himself." True, but now that I knew he was extorting business owners all over town, I felt compelled to stop him for more reasons than self-defense.

"He brings it all on himself. He's a dumbass."

"You say he thinks you're loyal to him?"

"Well, I once said it was lame that crusty old wolves were ruling the pack. I guess he took that to mean I wanted to be an undyingly loyal member of his new order."

"Lorenzo and my mom aren't crusty."

"They're old and totally ignorant about the way the human world works."

"Because they don't think werewolves should have much to do with the human world," I guessed. I'd never heard Lorenzo's opinions on the matter, but I well remembered my mother's, and she didn't seem to have changed much over the years.

"Yeah, but that's not practical. Humans are *everywhere*."

"I have noticed that."

"Anyway, just because I don't agree with their old-school way of thinking and ruling doesn't mean I want to support a dumbass or overthrow the leadership. I figure that'll happen eventually—someone's going to challenge Lorenzo for the pack because that's just how it works." Jasmine shrugged, appearing no more disturbed by the *way of the wolf* than my mother. "But I personally hope it won't be Augustus. He's a jerk. I wish *you* would rule. You lived among humans for so long that you must get them, and you still remember what it's like to be a wolf and what the pack needs."

"Females don't lead packs. They're the mates of the males who do. I don't have to tell you that werewolves are pretty traditional when it comes to family relations."

Jasmine snorted. "That's just because males are usually stronger. You can kick a lot of the guys' asses though." She looked wistfully at me, as if she could will a desire to lead the pack into me. "But you do need to watch out. Augustus was trying to rally everyone who came to that meeting to help him get you. Some of the family protested and said he needed to fight you fairly if he wanted you out of the pack—or dead."

"Advice he did not take to heart." I touched my maligned shoulder.

"No kidding. At the end of the meeting, he pulled aside several of his siblings, the ones that *didn't* say anything about fair fighting, and I caught a few words before they moved away. They said they're going to get rid of you, one way or another, as soon as they catch you without your protector. They're majorly salty about Duncan's arrival and resent you for conjuring him up."

"I had nothing to do with his arrival." If that vision could be believed, magic or destiny or something far beyond me had drawn Duncan, just as it had brought the wolf case up here to pack territory. "Though I'm delighted he's vexing Augustus."

"Me too. But they might go after him so it'll be easier to get to you."

That wouldn't come as a surprise to Duncan, but I made a mental note to warn him. He had enough trouble worrying about his creator; he didn't need Augustus gunning for him. But if Jasmine was right, Duncan's actions on my behalf almost ensured they would.

"Do you have the address for Augustus's house?" I asked.

He kept showing up at my home. Maybe it was time for me to visit him at his. I might be able to catch him off-guard there. Though, unless I wanted to outright kill him, I would have to come up with a plan to get him to confess to his nefarious doings. My attempts the night before had failed.

"I do," Jasmine said, "but some of his siblings hang out there too, so it's not a good spot where you can catch him with his pants down, if that's what you're thinking."

"I'm not sure yet what I'm thinking, but I promise it won't involve his pants." Unless I could get the alchemist Rue to make some delightfully horrible potion that I could fling if I did chance upon him with them down. She *had* mentioned an ability to afflict someone with genital warts. That probably wouldn't stop Augustus's life of crime, but I couldn't help but think it would improve him on some level. "I'll come up with something."

"Okay." Looking hopeful, Jasmine took her phone out and texted me an address.

Too bad my ally was MIA. I would have to come up with a plan on my own.

16

I DIDN'T WEAR THE GAS MASK TO CLEAN, BUT I *DID* LEAVE ALL THE doors and windows open as I scrubbed and sprayed. Smells of pets—and pet scat—were almost as difficult to get rid of as cigarette smoke, but at least the apartment didn't have any carpet. In most of the units, I'd long ago replaced that with durable vinyl floor planks. Despite Duncan's complaint about how they chilled his wolf flanks, they resisted stains and didn't trap odors. In my world, that made them practical.

Jasmine had watched me work for ten minutes before noting that my job wasn't that glamorous for a werewolf and losing interest. Before leaving, she'd polished off Bolin's coffee, proving they had similar tastes, preferring a dreadful amount of sugar in their espresso drinks. Maybe, if he plied her with mochas, she would look twice at him. Thus far, I hadn't seen any of the prospective tenants he'd attempted to flirt with return his interest. I wasn't sure they'd *known* he was flirting, especially when he'd started talking about spelling bees and word origins.

During a break, I wiped sweat from my brow and dialed the

number that Rue had left when she'd sent in an application for an apartment.

"Greetings, wayward werewolf," she answered on the second ring. "I've been hoping you would call. I grow weary of dealing with the—" she raised her voice, "—miscreant shits-for-brains that keep defiling my door."

"Are they... there now?" I imagined her leaning into the hallway for that last.

"There is fresh graffiti, and the grandma who waves her holy book at me just walked past. She is *not* holy."

"Those who leave menacing messages on people's doors rarely are." I grabbed a soapy rag to rub at suspicious marks on the trim but had already accepted that I would have to paint. The marks were barely noticeable next to all the nail holes, gouges, dents, and scrapes.

"*Exactly.* I told the landlord, and he blames me."

"Strange."

"Quite."

"Well, I called to let you know we have a vacated unit. I'm cleaning it now."

"That will be acceptable. I mind my own business and do not bother anyone. Unless one counts the misty vapors that filled the hallway recently and made those who passed through it itchy. They should be thankful. The vapor formula has a much more potent version."

I paused in my cleaning to eye the phone, starting to have second thoughts about offering Rue an apartment. Originally, I'd been thinking it would be handy to have a potion supplier nearby again, but I hadn't been taking the sublimation concoction lately. Did I actually *need* an alchemist? Maybe I should have talked to her landlord before offering her a unit.

"We don't have hallways here," was all I said. "The units have exterior doors."

"That is fine. In fact, that is preferable. When can I move in? I have four grandsons and two granddaughters that I can put to work packing."

"Lucky them."

"In my culture, it is an honor to serve your elders."

I had a feeling her neighbors would all chip in to see her leave too, but I didn't voice the thought. Silently, I told myself that having her nearby *would* be handy. Besides, she couldn't be any worse than the switch-plate thieves with their poorly trained cats.

"The apartment will be ready in four days." Normally, I would have said two, but painting took some time, and I had to allow for relatives interrupting my work with their efforts to kill me.

"I will be ready to move before the weekend. Goodbye."

After lowering the phone, I rotated stiff joints and thought longingly of my bed. That morning, by the time things had settled, I'd been too awake to go to sleep. I *had* dozed in the chair in the leasing office during the lunch hour until a tenant had come by to report a leaky showerhead. She'd caught me with my shoes on the desk, my head dangling over the arm rest, and drool at the corner of my mouth. But I'd had extra cartridges for the showers in the office and had done the repair on the spot, so she shouldn't have had a reason to complain. With the threat of the Sylvans selling the place looming, I didn't want to do anything that would give them an extra reason to want to bail on the property.

Beeping sounds floated in from the parking lot. That was probably the truck I'd ordered to pick up the furniture the Donovans had left behind. When I stepped outside, I found darkness creeping over the city once again, the encroaching night *almost* hiding a naked man jogging through the parking lot.

"Duncan," I blurted, sensing him before my eyes could identify him with certainty. Not that anyone else was likely to run naked through the parking lot while a big junk-hauling truck backed into a spot up front.

I wanted to run over and check on him—had he walked all the way back to Shoreline? I wished I'd known where he'd ended up. I could have picked him up.

But the junk guys were climbing out of their truck, so I first stopped to direct them. By the time I reached Duncan's van, he'd put on clothes, so I couldn't tell if he'd been injured.

"Are you okay?" I leaned through the open sliding door. "I have your other clothes in my truck."

"Are you keeping them hostage or is that a suggestion that I should retrieve them?" He was sitting on the bed, tying his shoes.

"The latter. I don't want them, unless you think I should keep them to use as dust rags."

"There was a Brioni sweater in the mix. Using it to dust would be egregious."

"Is that so?"

"It's cashmere."

"I bet that picks up fine particles well."

Duncan gave me an aggrieved look. "More appropriate would be if you kept everything tucked away in a drawer. Then, in the event of my death, you would have my clothing as mementos to cherish and look at any time you were pining for me."

He scraped his fingers through his wavy hair to comb it, as if removing any reminder of the great wild creature he'd been the night before. No, not *that* wild. He'd been scarier than he was in his wolf form, but he'd changed to help me, and he'd known he was doing it in the midst of all that roaring and raking with claws.

"They'd be more useful as dust rags," I said.

"You're a sentimental sort, aren't you?"

"As all werewolves are."

When Duncan stood, ducking to keep his head from hitting the bicycle mounted horizontally from the ceiling, he didn't appear to be favoring anything.

"You didn't answer if you're okay. My cousins sent you flying a few times, and then..." I held a hand out. *Then* I didn't know what had happened. Since his disappearance, I'd been assuming his creator's call had worked, summoning him back to the north.

"Their meager blows did little to affect me."

"What happened after that?" By now, I was used to him being evasive with me, but I wanted to know if he'd been horribly mentally tortured. Or... My gaze drifted to the scar on his forehead. Or if they'd done something to increase their ability to control him and he was, even now, serving their wishes. I decided to move the case out of the glove box in my truck later.

"It's a bit of a blur." Duncan sat on the bed again and patted it to offer me a spot. "A call even stronger than that of the moon drew me away from you. It started *during* the fight, but I was able to tamp down its pull while you were in danger. But once it was clear we'd gotten the upper hand... I couldn't resist anymore. I did try, but my body betrayed me. In that form, I seem particularly susceptible to magical compulsion. I kept trying to change to my wolf or human form, in case it would be easier to resist, but it wasn't until I reached those lavender fields that I was able to pause. I heard howling—the boy. My younger self."

I joined him in the van, but he looked out a window toward the north instead of at me.

"There was a warning in that howl," he continued, "and then... I'm not sure what happened, but a number of armored cars left the compound. I think those with the magical device were in one of them. For a moment, its hold on me faltered. I was able to change into a wolf, and then the pull of other magic affected me, the call of the moon. I took off to hunt, that instinct overriding the control magic." Duncan shrugged. "I'm not certain why the men departed at that moment, but I managed to leave the farm, satisfy the need to hunt, and return here. My paws—feet—are tired from all the miles I put on them though."

When he looked at me, I tried to appear supportive, not

worried or suspicious, but I couldn't help but think it had been awfully easy for him to escape. Why, after he'd been compelled to travel twenty miles or more had the compulsion lessened? It was hard to believe a howling eight-year-old could have been responsible for anything. Duncan had said it had been a blur. Was it possible he *hadn't* been able to stop when he reached the field? That he'd gone to his would-be masters, and Lord Abrams had done something to him? As I'd just been thinking? Even now, he could be theirs again.

"That was my day." Duncan slapped his palms on his thighs. "How was yours? Less eventful? I trust you got away from your cousins without more trouble?"

"For now. The rest of the night and day was fine." I yawned, reminded that I'd yet to sleep. "I cleaned out an apartment. Rue might be moving in this weekend."

"She may be an interesting tenant."

Movement outside a window drew my eye. The two young ghost hunters had come out and were setting up equipment between the parking lot and the greenbelt.

"They're *all* interesting tenants these days." I pointed out the window.

Duncan followed my gaze. "That looks like equipment for seeking out the paranormal. I wonder what they're looking for."

"Naked werewolves."

"If that's true, that meter should point toward this van."

"Undoubtedly. Do you want me to tell them?"

Duncan started to answer but shifted to look at something else, a delivery car pulling into the lot. Leaving it running, the driver got out with a package in her arms. She started toward the walkway heading to the buildings but paused to consider something on the label. Then she looked around the parking lot until she spotted the Roadtrek and headed toward it.

"You're getting mail here now?" I asked dryly, wondering if

he'd ordered more clothing. We'd both had a number of accidental changes lately.

"I didn't order anything. I didn't know it was possible to have packages delivered to a van."

The woman came closer, read *Full Moon Fortune Hunter* on the side of the Roadtrek, then knocked on the frame. She also noticed the open sliding door, her gaze drifting to the ceiling lamp that illuminated the interior, its yellowish-orange glow not quite the same as what one would get from a regular LED light.

"Greetings, my lady." Duncan hopped out and bowed to her.

She took a step back, looking more alarmed by his old-fashioned greeting than pleased by it. "I think I have something for you. What's your name?"

"Duncan Calderwood."

"Here you go." The delivery woman handed the package to him and headed back to her vehicle.

A piece of equipment in Duncan's van beeped a few times. She glanced back, then shifted from a walk to a jog.

"The apartment complex may be getting a reputation," I said sadly. "For quirk."

Or was it possible the delivery lady was on edge for another reason?

"That happens when you have atypical tenants." Box in one hand, Duncan waved toward the ghost hunters setting up their equipment.

"Yeah, *they're* the atypical ones."

He nodded and turned the box over, inspecting it from all sides.

"I don't suppose this is a gift of dark chocolate from you?" he said.

"I don't make enough money to afford a box of chocolate that large. Not of the superior quality brands that I like."

"I trust you wouldn't send me inferior quality."

"I wouldn't, no. If I wanted to insult you, I'd find other ways."

"Like using my sweaters for cleaning."

"That's just being practical. Dead werewolves don't need cashmere."

"Hm." Duncan pulled off the tape and opened the box. "Are you *sure* you didn't send this?"

I peered inside where a list of the contents rested among packing material nestled around a clear container of...

"Are those chocolates?" My nose caught the scent even before my eyes. Chocolates with... *bacon*?

Duncan picked up the handwritten list, a chocolatier's header on top, and read the listed contents aloud. "Chocolate-dipped bacon dusted with chopped pecans and flakes of sea salt."

I stared in surprise. I had a similar recipe, and we'd discussed such treats before.

"I didn't send them." I looked in the direction the delivery lady had gone, but she'd already driven out of the parking lot.

"I believe you, of course, but I can't imagine who else would have done so."

"I know. We were alone in my apartment when we talked about chocolate-dipped bacon, weren't we? It's not like someone would have overheard us. Even if they had, who else would have wanted to send you a gift?"

"I do have some sex appeal and have received unsolicited gifts from women in the past."

"Yeah, but you're fifty now. That can't happen *that* often."

"Really."

"Besides, who besides me would send you bacon and chocolate? That's..."

"Quirky?" He raised his eyebrows.

"Delicious. But specific." I took the paper from him and turned it over to read the ingredients.

Duncan lowered his nose to the box. "They smell fantastic.

Very fresh. After running through the night and day, I admit to being hungry."

"I wouldn't eat them."

"Because *you're* not ravenous."

"I've got your groceries in my fridge if you're hungry." I pointed to the label. "These were made with milk chocolate, not dark."

"I doubt that would affect my appreciation of them." He opened the lid.

"Yeah, but you know I didn't send it. I prefer dark chocolate." I held up a finger as he dug out a strip. "Someone who knows me and wanted you to *think* I sent these might not have been enough of a chocolate aficionado to know about or care about the difference."

"What are you saying?"

I took the strip from his fingers. "That we should have our new alchemist friend test it for substances *not* listed in the ingredients." I tossed it back into the box.

"You think it's *poisoned*?"

"I don't know, but there are people who want you dead." I told him about Jasmine's visit and the warning she'd given.

Duncan looked mournfully into the box.

"It would be particularly loathsome to poison chocolate." I typed the name of the chocolatier into my phone to look up the business. "Who would do something so vile?"

"I'd say the same kind of person who fantasizes about using an expensive cashmere sweater for dusting, but I know you didn't do it."

I didn't get any results back from the search. Someone had made up the company name.

"You're that certain I want to keep you alive, huh?" I showed Duncan the search results in case he and his empty stomach needed further convincing that the contents should be left alone.

"I trust that, one, you wouldn't defile chocolate so, and, two, you adore me and would never wish me harm."

"But especially one, right?"

"Quite."

With palpable reluctance, Duncan closed the box. After considering it thoughtfully, he placed it on the passenger seat in the van.

"I believe I will visit Rue," he said.

"She may press you into helping her pack."

"It would be worth it to find out if these are poisoned." His eyes narrowed to slits. "And who in the Seattle area might have purchased such a poison and from where."

"I hope she has answers for you."

"Do you want to come with me?"

"I'm tired. I need to go to sleep early tonight. And I definitely don't want to help someone pack."

"All right. I'll keep you updated."

As he drove off, I made a call.

"Hi, Luna," Jasmine answered.

"Hey. Is there anyone in the family, anyone who's on Augustus's side about things, who likes to bake? Or specifically make candies and other desserts?"

It wasn't a field that werewolves typically went into—butchery and meat smoking were more aligned with our natural talents—but that didn't mean that such things couldn't happen. Our kind weren't completely immune to the allure of sugar.

"Aunt Martina," Jasmine offered after a moment. "I wouldn't say she's on Augustus's side, but she makes things for the kids for birthdays and holidays."

"Like chocolates?"

"I think she's done some, yeah. Oh right. I remember. She does for sure. She has wolf molds that she uses."

"Is she friendly enough toward Augustus that if he asked her to make something, she would?"

"Probably. Especially if he brought her a haunch of meat along with the request."

"How about a side of bacon?"

"Uh, that might work. Why do you ask?"

I explained the mysterious box of chocolates.

"Aunt Martina wouldn't poison anyone," Jasmine said. "She's ethical. She doesn't even like it when her sons prey on ill or infirm animals on their hunts."

"Well, she might have wandered out of the kitchen while Augustus dumped poison in the chocolate."

"I can try to find out if she made anything for him."

"Okay, good. I appreciate it."

"Putting poison in chocolate would be a heinous act," Jasmine said.

"Tell me about it."

17

EXHAUSTED FROM THE PREVIOUS NIGHT'S ADVENTURES—
misadventures—I slept from eight p.m. until six a.m. I could have continued even longer than that, but my phone rang. It wasn't a number from my contacts, and I eyed it warily as I answered.

"Hello?"

"My wayward werewolf."

I blinked up at the ceiling a few times before the voice and greeting clicked. I would have to add Rue to my contacts.

"Luna or Ms. Valens works," I said. "And I'm not wayward. I've rediscovered my wolfness."

"Directly *after* I had to contact four suppliers and send your mate to scrounge all over the city and local wilds to acquire the ingredients for your potions."

"Yeah, sorry about that. Do you want them back?"

"I cannot think of anyone else who would desire such things."

"I have a cousin I wouldn't mind castrating."

"Oh, I have *numerous* potions for that. The ingredients aren't even difficult to find."

"I didn't mean literally, though I suppose that might improve his demeanor. At least make him less ambitious. But what I meant is that I could see sneaking some of the sublimation potion into whatever he drinks to steal his magic for a month."

Or for life. Augustus would doubtless be as much of a dick if he was fully human, but he would have less power with which to threaten people. I was positive Francisco, a type of werewolf himself, wouldn't cave to a mere human bullying him around.

"Slipping potions unannounced into people's beverages would be duplicitous and devilish behavior," Rue remarked.

"Yeah, you probably wouldn't want your potions used in that way," I said, though she hadn't sounded that judgmental.

"How you use your potions, once paid for, is up to you."

"Good to know. But I'd need something faster acting than the sublimation potion, anyway. What I really want is to make someone tell the truth. In front of witnesses. Or at least in front of my phone with the camera recording." I wondered if getting Francisco and the convenience-store owners to describe Augustus and explain his threats would satisfy the pack arbiter. Probably not. They were outsiders.

"You desire a truth elixir?" The judgment that hadn't been in Rue's tone before was there now. Did she find such magic distasteful?

"Uhm, do you have one?" I imagined Duncan pinning Augustus to the ground while we forced a potion down his throat. Maybe Jasmine would come with us and hold the camera.

"They are simple to make. They require only three ingredients and an insignificant application of magical talent. They're in the first chapter of almost every book of formulas that you'll find. Apprentice alchemists usually make a truth elixir in their first month of training, once they've moved from learning to source and gather ingredients to mixing components and applying magic."

I realized the judgment in her tone might have more to do with the simplicity of the formula than any condemnation for how it might be used. Apparently, she was a woman who liked challenging elixirs.

"Any chance you have a vial of it?" I asked.

"This is *not* what I called about, but I could acquire the ingredients and deign to make a truth elixir. You know, however, that my services aren't cheap."

I did not, in fact, know that. In addition to finding Rue, Duncan had paid for my sublimation potions. He hadn't mentioned their cost. Since he'd betrayed me, I hadn't felt compelled to pay him back for them.

"I charge a minimum of $400 an hour, plus travel expenses for ingredient acquisition."

"Damn, you cost more than a lawyer." I rolled out of bed and headed to the kitchen, feeling the need for an espresso to get through the rest of the conversation. Fortunately, my machine came on automatically in the morning, so it was preheated and ready to brew.

Rue sniffed. "Those who are competent in my profession are *much* rarer than lawyers, and I have more than forty years of experience." She lowered her voice to mutter, "As if you can't find a lawyer on every street corner, plying his wares."

"They're not the profession I usually think of as plying from street corners, but I'll admit they are easier to find than alchemists."

"*Of course* they are. It requires no magical blood to file paperwork. My kind are *exceedingly* rare, and I'm in high demand from those who need my services. I was on the verge of raising my rates to $500 to finance my move."

"I thought your grandkids were boxing everything up. Won't they work for pizza?"

"A truck must be rented. And we have not discussed rates at your complex. I had assumed that moving to the suburbs would be more affordable, but it's possible you charge a premium for an apartment without miscreants constantly leaving graffiti."

I started to assure her that Shoreline was less expensive than Seattle, and I'd throw in a graffiti-free door at no extra charge, but I didn't have money budgeted for truth potions. It occurred to me to negotiate.

"Our rent is quite reasonable," I said, "and I'm authorized to provide discounts to seniors and veterans. Have you ever served in the armed forces?"

"In my homeland in my youth, I attended the Alchemy Academy, which included learning to defend the nearby littoral village in case of an assault on the paranormal beings living there. We learned to fight with staves, explosives, and magical munitions."

"Wow, sounds exotic."

"That particular part of the country was, due to more than the typical amount of magic lingering in the earth, yes."

"Well, if you could give me a deal on a truth elixir, I'd be willing to check *yes* on the veteran box. I'll put you down under Coast Guard." Littoral meant by the water, didn't it? "That would give you ten percent off each month." I hit the button for the coffee grinder and then moved away from the machine so it wouldn't drown out my voice. "And then I'm guessing you're over sixty-five. I can give you another ten percent off each month for being a senior." I remembered that the Sylvans were contemplating selling the property. Hopefully, the next owners would honor the existing leases—and not look too closely at applicants' veteran status.

"I will bring you four potions. Do you also require an antidote for the poison that the old-world werewolf brought by last night?"

"I— What?" I'd been so distracted by thoughts of truth elixirs that I hadn't asked why Rue had called. I hurried to pull my shots, needing the bracing caffeine even more now.

"He did not appear to be ailing when he came to my apartment, but it is a slow-acting poison. Likely, he or she who left it wished to avoid being associated with it. He said it came in an edible delectable?"

"Yeah, chocolate-dipped bacon."

"Interesting. For a werewolf, I would have assumed a haunch of meat. I did not know they craved sweets."

"I've taught him the delights of dark chocolate. He didn't eat any, so we shouldn't need antidotes, but maybe I should have you make some in case whoever sent it strikes again."

I didn't know why I said *whoever*. I knew exactly who'd done it. The night before, when I'd called Jasmine, I'd known. Nobody else would poison Duncan to get him out of the way.

"You will include three months' rent-free in exchange for a four-pack of the antidote? To go along with the truth serum?"

I managed to scowl at my phone and swallow a mouthful from my steaming Americano at the same time. "I don't own this place, Rue. It's not like I'll make any more from getting a new tenant."

Especially a new wheeling-and-dealing tenant who wanted more discounts than a bargain shopper on double-coupon day.

"You do not receive commissions?"

"No. I'm on salary."

"Two months," Rue said firmly. "I am certain a large apartment complex regularly offers discounts to secure new tenants. Especially in the winter."

She wasn't wrong, but I squinted suspiciously at the phone. "How often have you moved apartments, Rue?"

How often had she been *forced* to move apartments by neighbors and landlords suspicious of her witchy—alchemy—ways?

"I frequently enjoy a change of scenery."

"Uh-huh. Okay, the discounts I mentioned earlier, and two months' free rent with a two-year lease. But you'll need to pony up a damage deposit. I've been in your apartment. It reeks of incense, burned cauldron mixings, and chicken feet."

I took another long swig of my coffee while waiting for her to argue further.

"That is fair," was all she said. "I will prepare the potions before I finish packing. I believe... Yes, I have not yet boxed up the ingredients I will need."

"Thank you. Uhm, Rue? Just so I know, would the poison have killed someone who consumed it?"

"Oh yes. It's very deadly. Even though it doesn't act quickly, it's magical in nature and proliferates in the bloodstream. It's designed to kill even hearty paranormal individuals with greater immune systems than mundane human beings."

"I was afraid of that."

"The antidote, delivered in time, destroys the poison before the proliferation can turn exponential."

I shuddered. "That antidote sounds like something everyone should have in the cabinet."

"Everyone with enemies who have access to poison makers, yes."

How sad that I'd become such a person of late. Even though I'd enjoyed answering the call of the wolf again, and hunting under the silver moonlight, a part of me missed the days when my greatest enemies had been the parents from my sons' rival soccer teams. In a hissy fit of frustration and despair over a loss, one mom had thrown a rice-crispy treat at our coach that had bounced off his shoulder and hit me in the head. I'd recovered fully from the ordeal.

While I dressed, I finished my Americano and brewed two more drinks, putting them in my insulated to-go cups. With the beverages in hand, I headed out to Duncan's van to warn him to throw away the desserts, if he hadn't already. Given the way he'd drooled over them the night before, he might have been waiting with hope for a negative result.

His sliding door opened before I knocked on the van. Shirtless, with his hair mussed, he smiled brightly at me—or possibly the coffee cups.

"Is one of those for me?"

"Yup."

His eyelids drooped. "I adore you."

"I'd be delighted, but I think you would have said that to Bolin, too, if he'd brought you caffeine."

"Possibly, but I wouldn't have lowered my eyelids sexily at him." Duncan accepted my offered cup and took a deep drink. He'd had a rough couple of days too.

"That's good. From what I've seen of his tastes, sexily lowered eyelids of the male variety might alarm him."

"I didn't think the kid ever shared his coffee anyway." Duncan hopped out to join me in the parking lot. Maybe because his bed was a mess—yes, he *must* have had a rough night—he didn't feel proper offering it as a seat. "When he wanders in from the parking lot, he's always clutching his cups like they're ancient Incan treasures."

"He needs a lot of fortification to start the workday at eight. But if you're a cute girl, he might share."

Of the various *cute girls* I'd seen him moon-eye, he'd actually only offered coffee to Jasmine. He'd given me one the morning I'd come in with twigs and leaves and moss in my hair, but it hadn't been the fancy whipped-cream-topped mocha.

"Or if you slept in the woods," I added.

"That applies to me often."

"I suppose the van is quite the improvement over waking up in a bed of ferns."

His eyelids drooped again. "It depends who I wake up *with* in the ferns." A fond smile crept across his face as he considered me.

"Are you thinking of the time you woke up with your hand on my boob?"

"I think of it often. Is that inappropriate?"

"Completely."

"Do you mind?"

"Not as much as I should."

His eyelids drooped further. Damn if he didn't look sexy, especially with his shirt off.

He also looked like he was about two seconds from inviting me inside, mussed bed or not, so that we could explore each other's bodies without any of my relatives nearby. For a moment, I considered accepting such an offer, but... I needed to deal with Augustus and ensure the complex wouldn't be threatened again by werewolves or thugs hopped up on potions. It was only a few days until my son arrived, and who knew the Sylvans' timeline and how seriously they were considering selling the apartments? The gravity of everything I needed to do weighed on me.

"Rue called me," I said. "Your chocolates are poisoned."

Duncan nodded without surprise. "She called me too. I understand you're a tough negotiator, but she'll be moving in this weekend. It'll be handy to have her close for all the future times I need gifts analyzed."

"Are you planning to stay in my parking lot long-term enough to receive a lot of dubious gifts?"

"My sex appeal and fame as a treasure-hunting YouTuber ensures a steady stream of such."

"Given that you don't have a mailing address, I'm skeptical of that. It's a wonder that delivery person found you."

"Your cousins know exactly where I am. I assume you believe they were responsible?"

"Yeah." I told him about the family dessert maker. "I've got Rue preparing antidotes for the poison."

"You didn't think I'd be able to resist eating the chocolates even knowing they're poisoned?"

"I want to be prepared in case Augustus tries again. In the

meantime, you might want to avoid accepting food from random people off the street."

"I'm currently drinking coffee that *you* gave me."

"I'm from an apartment, not off the street. You're probably safe."

"True. And I trust you want to keep me alive. Were I to die horribly at your feet, nobody as handsome as I would fantasize over fondling your anatomy."

"That would be heartrending."

"Yes." His lazy smile filled me with warmth and made me think again of trysts in his van, but the roar of multiple motorcycles came from the street.

I grimaced. "What now?"

Two riders without helmets drove Harleys slowly past the parking lot. I didn't think they were any of the men who'd troubled us before—facing off against Duncan had to have deterred some of those guys—but they had the same vibe, straight down to the drugged bloodshot eyes. The pair didn't scope out the cars as if they had vandalism in mind. Instead, they looked straight at Duncan and me, holding our gazes for long moments before they rode out of view.

"Were they to give me gifts, I would not consume them," Duncan said. "No matter how appetizing."

I shook my head, thoughts of morning interludes replaced by bleakness. I had a feeling the local criminal element knew we'd been responsible for stopping that robbery and didn't appreciate having me in the neighborhood nearly as much as the store owners did.

18

My phone rested on the kitchen table next to eight vials of liquid. Four were red and four bluish-purple. They weren't labeled, but when Rue had brought them by, at the same time requesting a tour of her future home, she'd made sure to identify which were the truth elixirs and which the antidotes for the poison. After sniffing disdainfully only a few times at the half-cleaned apartment—fortunately, after my previous day's work and the removal of the stained and odiferous furniture, it didn't look or smell that bad—she'd departed, looking cheerful.

With the potions delivered, I had a plan, but each time I reached for my phone, sweat broke out on my palms and I paused. What if this didn't work? I wasn't a thespian.

"I only have to fool Augustus," I told myself. "He's not that bright."

I was about to dial his number when a knock at the door startled me. Duncan? No, I sensed Jasmine.

Worried something had happened to Mom, I hurried to answer.

This time, Jasmine wasn't in her wolf form and noshing a

rabbit on my threshold. She stood in fitted exercise pants and a midriff shirt that left a couple of inches of her abdomen showing.

"Are you... on your way to yoga?" I wished something innocuous had brought her by and she'd only popped in because she was in the neighborhood.

"Zumba, actually. But I stopped by to tell you I talked to Aunt Martina, and she did, at Augustus's request, make bacon dipped in chocolate. She said she didn't see him do anything to it but, when I pressed her, she admitted he'd been alone in the kitchen when someone had rung her doorbell. She also said it had been weird that Augustus had made the request because he never had before. Apparently, he told her it was a *gift*, but he's not known for giving gifts."

"I'll bet he's not." I nodded to her. "Thanks for letting me know."

Jasmine looked around.

"Is there something else?" I wondered why she hadn't called to deliver that information.

"I thought if I saw that guy—your intern, right?—I'd ask him where he got that mocha. It was *so* good."

"Yes, Bolin is my intern, and I'm sure he would be delighted to tell you." I glanced at the time on my phone. "He should still be here. If you saw the SUV in a bubble out front, he's here."

"That's his car?"

"Yup."

"What's the weird bubble for? It didn't look antitheft. I could pop it easily." Jasmine crooked her index finger and made a claw-poking motion.

"It's to deter bird poop. Or... I guess more to stop the droppings from reaching the paint. From what I've seen of the bubble, it's as much of a target as the SUV."

"That's weird. I guess the staff spots *are* under a bunch of trees."

"Trees that are near bird feeders, yes. I have some tenants that will put food out for anything furred or feathered. I'm surprised nobody threw a pound of frozen ground beef at you when you sauntered through as a wolf."

Jasmine blinked a few times at the imagery. "My instincts told me to avoid humans on my way here."

"Because you didn't know about the wildlife-feeding tenants."

"I might come back for venison."

"Do you want me to put up a memo on the community board?"

"No, I prefer to hunt my own food. Anyway, I might see if I can find that guy—Bolin—before I leave."

"He'll be delighted to talk to you."

And her bare midriff.

"What are you going to do about Augustus? If you're going to strangle him, I'd like to watch."

"I have a plan to get a confession out of him."

I remembered that I'd envisioned Jasmine recording it from nearby. Would she be game for that?

"Strangling him might accomplish that," she said.

"His neck is too thick for me to get my hands around."

Not to mention that Augustus would kick my ass if I faced off against him while we were in human form. As a wolf, I was his match, but as a man... he could probably crush me by sitting on me.

"Do you want help?"

"With the strangulation?"

Jasmine laughed. "With your plan. When I was over at his house, he called my dad a dweeb. I don't know *why* he thinks I'm on his side."

"Because he's an idiot with the persuasive power of a blobfish."

"Dad *is* a dweeb, but only my mom, my sister, and I get to call him that. And only in a lovingly teasing kind of way."

"I actually could use some help."

It was nice of her to volunteer.

"I'm going to try to arrange a meeting with him to enact my plan," I added. "I could use a videographer."

"I can do that. Just let me know when you find out a time. I'm not doing anything after my class tonight."

"I'll call if this works out. Thanks."

Jasmine waved and departed. Alone again, I fortified myself with a square of dark chocolate, then pulled up a recording app on my phone. I'd had to sift through a lot of programs to find one that didn't announce to the person on the receiving end that the call was being recorded. Once it was running, I dialed the phone.

Augustus answered so promptly that I wondered if he'd expected my call.

Summoning all the acting power I had, I yelled, "You poisoned him, you asshole!"

It wasn't as hard as I thought to sound angry. I *was* angry and tired of dealing with relatives who couldn't mind their own business and had decided to hate me because of my personal choices, choices that had nothing to do with them.

"Is he dead?" Augustus asked without passion.

"You know he's not. Not yet. It acts slowly, doesn't it?"

"Are you recording this?"

"Yes, and I've got the cops standing right next to me listening to you on speaker phone."

Augustus snorted. "That's a lie. They don't give a shit about our kind. If they believe we exist at all."

"Duncan doesn't have anything to do with your feud with me. You had no right to try to *assassinate* him."

"He's been interfering with our *feud*, as you call it, since day one. What he sees in you and why he bothers, I can't guess."

"I'm a good lay, asshole."

"You must be."

"Is there an antidote?"

Augustus didn't answer. Maybe he hadn't expected that question. Maybe he had no idea.

"*Is* there?" I yelled, as if I was losing it. I took an audible deep breath. "A witch I talked to who knows about poisons said there might be."

"Yes." Augustus sounded like he'd decided that on the spot. With a croon in his voice, he added, "How much is it worth to you?"

"I can't let him die. He never should have been involved."

"Maybe you should have thought about that before bringing him into pack territory."

"Do you have the antidote? What do you want for it?"

"What are you offering?" Augustus asked softly, smugly. Like he was baiting a trap and luring me in, and we both knew it.

"What do you want? Me dead?"

"To be honest, I'm more partial to the idea of *him* dead. You won't be a problem to deal with if he's not around. How the hell did he become a bipedfuris anyway?"

I wanted to say I'd been in the process of kicking his ass when we'd been fighting one-on-one, so I had to be more of a *problem* than he thought. But insults weren't going to get me what I wanted.

"Killing him isn't acceptable," I said. "Name your price for the antidote."

"The ivory box."

I didn't have to manufacture a growl. I'd known he wanted that.

"*And* your mother's medallion after she passes."

"You don't want much, do you?"

"Neither of those things should be yours anyway."

"They're not *yours* either."

"Nope, but I'm going to take them. Just like I'm going to take the pack."

Hell, maybe he would give me enough to hand the arbiter without an in-person video recording. But I needed more than this. His ambition to take over the pack wasn't a secret. Mom had already talked about it. Everyone probably knew about it. I needed more out of him, especially since the pack would consider me, the female who'd disappeared for decades, an unreliable witness.

What I wanted and believed would work to sway the elders was Augustus admitting he was acting like a mafia boss out there and making a bad name for the Savagers. And I wanted it in a video confessional that I could show to everyone.

"You'll have to talk to my mom if you want the medallion," I said, "but I agree to trade the wolf case for the antidote."

"I want the case and for you to promise to hand over the medallion to me once your mother passes. *She's* not going to give it to me. We already know that."

"I thought you wanted it for your wife, not yourself. It's for female werewolves, you know."

"I'm getting it for her. I'm a good husband."

"Uh-huh." I hadn't seen his wife during any of our confrontations, which made me wonder how much time they actually spent together. Hadn't Mom said they were separated? Maybe his wife had learned after marrying him what a douchebag he was. "I need the antidote right away. Where do you want to do the exchange? Someplace neutral."

"Come to my house tonight."

"That's not *neutral*. I want to meet at a park."

"My house is where the antidote is."

"You don't have *pockets*?"

"The vials are big."

Yeah, right.

"If you want the antidote," he continued, "you'll come here. Eight p.m."

I ground my teeth, but if I argued too much, Augustus might

suspect Duncan wasn't in that bad of a state. If I did anything but give in to his demands, it would be suspicious.

"I need the antidote right away," I said, putting a desperate hitch in my voice.

"Tonight is soon enough," Augustus said firmly. "That poison takes a couple of days to kill. Besides, I'm having a little gathering tonight, and I have to get the place ready."

"You're afraid to meet me alone?"

"I don't know what schemes you're concocting."

"*You're* the one who poisoned my friend, and you accuse *me* of scheming?" My palms were so damp my phone almost slipped out of my grip. I was scheming my brains out.

"Bring the case tonight. Eight p.m. If you don't have it with you, you're not getting past security."

"What, have you got a castle with an alligator-filled moat?"

"Something like that."

I remembered the magical defenses at my mom's place—and my painful realization that he'd been behind them, or he'd at least colluded with whoever had installed them. That same person—probably another of my cousins—might have littered the grounds of his lake house with them.

"I'll have the case," I said. "You just make sure you have the antidote."

"I do, but if you bring the bipedfuris, you're also not getting in."

"I need to give him the antidote as soon as I get it."

"You're *not* getting in with him. I'll be at the gate to check in person."

"Fine," I growled.

"And I have magical devices that will let me know if someone with old-world werewolf blood tries to sneak in."

"He's not sneaking anywhere. You poisoned him. He can barely get out of bed."

"What a shame. Deal's off if you bring him." Augustus hung up.

I stopped the recording and lowered the phone. "Part One of my plan is complete."

Too bad I hadn't been able to get him to agree to meet on neutral territory. I worried this wouldn't go well.

19

After I finished cleaning the vacated apartment, returned inquiries by phone and email, and helped a couple of tenants with problems, I called it a day and headed to the parking lot. The Roadtrek had recently appeared there, back from wherever Duncan had gone during the day. Magnet fishing, probably.

Since he'd been gone, I hadn't yet had a chance to run my plan by him, but I'd called Jasmine and given her the details. I'd also asked her, in the event of my death, to warn my mother that Augustus was after her medallion and that she shouldn't trust her driveway alarms.

If Mom had a phone, like a civilized person, I could have shared that warning myself, but there wasn't time to drive up to her cabin. Sammamish was in a different direction, and I planned to show up at Augustus's lake house early. Ideally before those he'd invited to his shindig arrived. I had a feeling his guests would be his loyal lackeys, happy to jump in and clobber me.

While I'd been working, I'd had second and third thoughts about agreeing to go to Augustus's house. I wished I'd come up with something else. But if I'd negotiated too much, when

Duncan's life supposedly hung by a thread, my cousin would have been suspicious. He'd believed he'd had all the leverage. I wasn't sure that belief was wrong.

I knocked on Duncan's sliding door.

"Do you have any grenades I can borrow?" I asked when he opened it.

His eyebrows rose. "One doesn't typically *borrow* grenades. They're difficult to return once they've been used."

"It's possible I won't need to use them."

"Where are you taking them?"

"To my cousin's house." I showed him the map I'd pulled up of the address. It was a long lakeside lot with a dock extending into the water. An ivy-covered stone wall and gate blocked Street View from seeing the house, but it appeared large on the satellite imagery. Maybe it *was* a castle.

"You'll need them then."

"Yeah, probably so. I'll rephrase. Do you have any grenades that I can *have*? I can pay." Not sure how much grenades cost, I delved into my purse and sifted through my budgeting envelopes. After hesitating, I held up the one labeled ENTERTAINMENT.

"Is that what blowing up your cousin would fall under?" Duncan asked.

"It might. It's either that or MISCELLANEOUS, but I never put much money in that one. I prefer to categorize carefully and accurately. That envelope has always seemed like an excuse to be undisciplined."

"What a terrible thing to be." Duncan's eyes twinkled as he waved for me to put the envelopes away. "Unfortunately, I can't be your grenade dealer. I haven't had a chance to replenish my supply."

"You only had two?" I peered into his van. "I guess space is at a premium in a house on wheels."

"Quite true. Are you breaking into a home on a lake?" He

pointed at the map on the phone. "As I mentioned to you before, I *do* have underwater demolitions."

"Do those have a pin you can pull as you hurl them over a gate?"

"No. You set them, then swim away and detonate them remotely. They're much more sophisticated than grenades."

"I don't need sophisticated for Augustus."

"A bear trap and a club ought to be sufficient for him. But are you certain you wouldn't want to blow up his dock? And is that a boat house attached? Goodness, such a palatial home for a werewolf."

"Yeah, our kind aren't supposed to care that much about money and mansions and luxury lifestyles. We're furry Spartans, if not troglodytes. We howl at the moon and pee to mark our territory."

"I may resemble that remark," Duncan murmured, eyeing the satellite imagery as we spoke.

"I know you do. I have a nose." I tapped it and nodded significantly toward the greenbelt, well aware that he'd marked territory back there.

"I was attempting to ward off your odious cousins."

"And let other males know there's a female here that you're interested in?"

"Of course. Are you flattered?"

"More than I should be," I said.

His smile was smug. "May I assume that when you visit Augustus in his oversized abode, you would like some company?"

I hesitated. I *did* want his company, but...

"He said not to bring you." I summed up the phone conversation, then added, "I'm asking Jasmine to come. I don't think Augustus will object to her, and I need someone to hold the camera while I throttle the truth out of him."

Duncan blinked slowly, looking stunned. "What you *need* is

someone to walk at your side and fight with you when he breaks his word and launches a legion of werewolves at you."

"I probably do need that, but he won't let me in if I show up with you, and he said he can detect you. Throwing you in the back of my truck under a blanket won't work."

"What if I wear SCUBA gear and come in via the dock? I could blow up the boathouse as a distraction on my way in."

"I..." That actually sounded fantastic. "That would irk him."

"*Good.*"

"I would love to have you with me, Duncan, but I'm concerned about you, not just about my plan working. He's gunning for you, and..."

"I can avoid licking any candy he hands me when I show up."

"That's not it. Or not *all* of it." I looked frankly into his eyes. "The last couple of times we've fought together, you've turned into the bipedfuris and, shortly after, you've fallen under the spell of Lord Abrams."

"I'm certain it was a coincidence last time. He and Radomir couldn't have known I was changing at that moment."

"But they've been trying to call you for days, right?"

"They have."

"Even *I've* felt the magic. You're more susceptible to it when you're in that form, aren't you?"

Duncan hesitated and looked away.

I waited, my gaze locked on his face. I had a hunch I was right about this.

"I am more susceptible to control in that form. When Abrams was raising me, he had plenty of time to study me, to figure out my strengths and weaknesses. In that form, I'm strongest and most dangerous but also the least... in control. Even without a magical compulsion, I'm savage when I'm the two-legs. As you saw." He grimaced and only glanced at me before staring at the pavement.

"I saw you protect me last time." I didn't mention that he'd attacked me the first time. Abrams had been standing scant feet away then, that device pointed right at Duncan. "And hurl one of my cousins into a tree. That was nice."

"It was savage."

"Savagely nice from my point of view. And they deserved it."

"That I'll agree with." Duncan met my gaze. "Look, I don't have to take that form tonight. I can be myself as a human or turn into a wolf. Don't go into your cousin's lair with only a girl for help."

"Jasmine is more than a girl; she's one of us."

"Not one who fights a lot. I can tell. You need a *strong* ally. And a plan."

"I have a plan."

A hesitant knock sounded on the other side of the van, and I sensed Bolin.

"And that's it," I added, then stepped around the front of the van, startling him. His leather messenger bag was slung over one shoulder and slipped down to his elbow when he jumped.

"Is *he* going with you too?" Duncan had followed me around the hood and gave me an aggrieved look.

"Going where?" Bolin asked warily, pushing the strap back onto his shoulder.

"Into the lair of deadly wolves," Duncan said.

"He's not," I said at the same time as Bolin issued an emphatic, "No."

"I brought something for Luna," Bolin added, glancing at Duncan before looking at me. "Do you want it, uhm, with witnesses?"

Duncan folded his arms over his chest.

"It's fine," I said. "He's my ally. He's going to provide a distraction out back while I enter the lair through the gate." I smiled at Duncan, hoping that would make him happy. Even if I had doubts about relying on him when he could be called off by those who wanted to be his masters at any time, I thought he *could* be useful for creating a distraction. "He has SCUBA gear and underwater demolitions," I added.

"Yes." Duncan lifted his chin.

"Underwater demolitions?" Bolin asked dubiously.

"Explosives," Duncan said.

Bolin rolled his eyes. "I *know* what demolitions are. The word is originally from the Latin verb *moliri,* which means to build, and the prefix *de-* which means to undo. I was just surprised because wolf lairs presumably aren't underwater and, when you first spoke of the home as such, I didn't think it was a metaphor. Due to, well..." He waved vaguely at us.

Figured out the werewolf thing, had he? I'd assumed he had.

"Well, it is a literal wolf's lair, I suppose," I said, "but it's also a big lakefront mansion."

"I intend to *undo* the dock and boathouse," Duncan said. "And ideally the owner."

"That sounds violent," Bolin murmured.

"It's in our blood," I said.

"I believe that." Bolin lifted the flap of his bag. "I'm not sure you need my formulas if you've got explosives, but, per your request, I acquired these for you."

He held out four vials of green glowing liquid and two swirling blue-green spheres of compressed powder. If I'd seen them on a store shelf, I would have thought them bath bombs.

"Those make a sticky mess on the floor when they dissolve." Bolin pointed to the spheres. "Sticky enough to ensnare people, like Entangling Vines in *Destiny Wields a Sword*."

"I haven't played that yet." I wasn't sure why I said *yet.* I'd blown up some bad guys in my sons' video games when they'd been growing up, but my special talent had been running my avatar off cliffs and dying before the enemies showed up.

Bolin stared at me as if he couldn't believe it.

"I'm saving the delight for retirement," I said.

"Are you *sure* you're not a Boomer?"

"Positive. Are the vials the same thing that we saw you use in the parking lot the day we met? That threw up vapors and stung the eyes of the motorcycle thugs?"

"Yes."

"Those tricks don't sound like they'll be that effective against werewolves," Duncan said. "Wouldn't you prefer to blow up the house and your cousins with it?"

"I know you're a nomadic treasure-hunter who's new to this country," I said, "but both of those things are crimes here."

"But blowing up the boathouse is okay?"

No, but since he'd offered... "I think that's a petty crime. The penalties would be less... penal."

Bolin's eyebrows rose. "I shouldn't, as a law-abiding citizen, be listening to this conversation."

"Probably not. Thank you for bringing these." After taking the vials and bath bombs, I shooed him away.

When Bolin was out of earshot, Duncan said, "Your cousins are going to keep coming after you unless you get rid of them permanently."

"I'm going to force Augustus to confess to his bad behavior, not kill him. You can't *murder* family."

"They're trying to murder you."

"Because they don't consider me family anymore due to the choice I made to leave."

"Don't make it sound like this is *your* fault when they're the arseholes."

I shrugged. "I'm not, but... I used to babysit Augustus and several of the others. I can't kill them. I've seen them in their Underoos."

Duncan blinked. "Their what?"

"Superhero underwear. Didn't Lord Abrams give you any when you were growing up?"

"He did not."

"What an insufficient parental figure he was."

"I won't argue that."

"Capes were even involved," I said. "I know you're a fan of capes."

"Of all the people in the world who *don't* deserve to wear superhero undergarments, your brutish cousins are at the top of the list."

"I agree, but I can't plot to kill them. It's bad enough…" I waved a hand at the parking lot where we'd battled Radomir's thugs. Where I'd lost my humanity and *killed* some of them. I wasn't sure I wouldn't yet be discovered and brought up on charges for that. My karma had been twisted in knots, dropped on the ground, and stomped on.

"When people try to kill you, Luna, you have to kill them back. You can't wait idly around until they poison your chocolate."

I blew out a slow breath, admitting he wasn't entirely wrong, but… "Like Bolin, I'm a law-abiding citizen with ties to this place and the human world. I have to live by their laws. *Our* laws. Even if I didn't have a moral issue with killing family… I don't want to end up in jail. I'm going to gather evidence—a confession—and let the pack elders handle my cousins."

Duncan's eyes narrowed. He'd stood up for me a number of times, jumping into fights that weren't his, and his mulish expression worried me. He wasn't contemplating doing the deed and taking the fall for me, was he? I didn't want that.

"I'll allow that human laws and law enforcement haven't been sufficient to help me with my family werewolf problems," I said, "but let me go through the proper channels with the pack before we consider anything drastic. Like I said, I'll get a confession and show it to the arbiter. Lorenzo is in charge, and, if they're motivated, the elders are strong enough to band together and get Augustus and whoever stands with him to leave."

"*Usually*, you can get bullies to back down by punching them in the nose and showing them you're not afraid, but those blokes..." Duncan shook his head. "I don't understand their animosity."

"I think it's that we've so *successfully* punched them in the noses. Augustus might have scorned me before, but now he hates me. And you."

Duncan waved toward my phone, though the screen had gone dark, the map disappearing. "Send me the address, okay? And tell me what time you want me to be there. I'll find a nearby public dock and swim over."

"Okay. And you don't really have to blow up anything. An explosion out in the water would be a fine distraction."

"He sent me poisoned chocolates. I'm annihilating his dock and his boathouse, then peeing on every square inch of his smoldering waterfront."

I hadn't realized Duncan had a vindictive streak, but Augustus had, in sending the poison, made it personal for Duncan.

"I trust you'll turn into a wolf first for the latter," was all I said.

"We'll see how irked I get."

"Make sure to give yourself time to remove your SCUBA gear before changing. I assume your wetsuit and tanks are expensive. You wouldn't want them to disappear into the ether."

"That's the truth." Duncan took a deep breath, exhaled slowly, and shook his arms, as if to loosen tense muscles. "What time?"

"Eight p.m. I need to grab a few things and pick up Jasmine on the way." I stepped forward and clasped his hands. "Thanks for helping me."

"You're welcome."

"We'll go hunting together somewhere exotic after all this is resolved."

"Exotic? Like South America? Africa?"

"I was thinking Leavenworth," I said, naming the tourist town on the east side of the mountains. I was fairly certain they had snow over there now and envisioned chasing game through a wintry landscape.

"I don't know where that is."

"A couple hours that way." I pointed east. "It's a cute Bavarian-themed town on a river surrounded by woods."

"When you said exotic, I envisioned us stalking giraffes and elephants in the Serengeti."

"Leavenworth is more in my budget. And it has a fudge shop."

"*Almost* as enticing as a giraffe."

"Yes. And it involves less fur getting in your mouth."

He snorted. "You're a quirky werewolf."

"I think we've established that we both are."

"Yes." Duncan squeezed my hands, then kissed me on the cheek, letting his lips linger before drawing back. He gave me a long look, like he wanted to do more than deliver a parting kiss, but he released me with determination in his eyes and headed for the driver's seat of his van.

Something about that determination made me uneasy. Again, I worried he might be willing to take out Augustus—if not every belligerent cousin I had—and accept the ramifications on my behalf.

Shaking my head, I went to my apartment to grab the rest of my potions and the wolf case before heading to my truck. For Duncan's sake, I would pick up Jasmine early and be at Augustus's house by 7:30. The moon willing, we could resolve everything before Duncan arrived.

20

MY STOMACH WAS CHURNING BY THE TIME I REACHED REDMOND TO pick up Jasmine. She still lived on her parents' property, in an ADU in the backyard, and was waiting for me when I pulled into the driveway. The lights were on in the main house, a 1960s rambler that was modest for the area, though it occupied a large treed lot that made it appealing to my werewolf senses.

"I'm excited to help you get your comeuppance on Augustus," Jasmine said as she slid into the passenger seat of my truck.

"Did you tell your parents where you're going tonight?" I hoped this wouldn't get her in trouble. Her mom had been helping my mom keep an eye on me over the years, so I doubted her parents wanted to see me slain by Augustus, but that didn't mean they would support a break-in and forced confession.

"I'm twenty-four, graduated, and a strong and independent werewolf woman. I go where I wish, when I wish."

"Uh-huh. When do you need to be home?"

"Unless there's a hunt, I have a one a.m. curfew." Jasmine wrinkled her nose. "*Aurora* doesn't have a curfew. She moved out last summer though. I'm saving to buy a condo, so I won't have *rules* to follow anymore, but I don't want to throw money away on rent, so it's going to take a while."

"One a.m. is a reasonable curfew."

"I guess. I can't play my music loud past nine though." She sighed dramatically, then turned on the truck's radio.

"I think condos have similar rules. HOAs are as bad as parents."

"Ugh, I know. Mom is in real estate. This truck doesn't have CarPlay or anything?"

"You're lucky it doesn't have punch buttons for the programmed stations. I would have gotten an even older truck if I hadn't been doing Uber on the side."

"Anything older than this would be valuable because it's a classic."

"Not all old cars are classics. Trust me." I brought up the navigation on my phone and followed the directions, heading south, toward Lake Sammamish and Augustus's house on the east side of it. "If you want true independence, you could buy a duplex and live in one side and rent out the other half."

"Duplexes are more expensive than condos. I'd be saving forever."

Since I'd been saving for my future fourplex for ages, I couldn't argue with that.

"Here we go." Jasmine found a station booming rap and turned up the volume. "This will help us get into the mood for storming a castle."

"You think so?"

"Yeah, this station plays classic rap. Good stuff."

Insane Clown Posse came on with "Under the Moon." I found the lyrics a little too apropos for my earlier thoughts about Duncan and was relieved when the song was over.

"What's the plan?" Jasmine held up her phone. "I'm ready to record, but how are you going to get him to confess to everything?"

I waved at the vials of potions rattling in the cup holder. "I have a number of truth elixirs. I intend to force, sneak, or otherwise inveigle one down his gullet. If any of my other cousins are around, I might do the same to them. They could be less stubborn about spilling their guts."

"But you don't want me to help you fight?" Jasmine looked at me. "I don't doubt that you can take Augustus one-on-one—"

I snorted since Augustus couldn't, as far as I'd seen, fight *anyone* by himself. He probably didn't even take a leak without one of his siblings holding his hand.

"—but he's not usually there alone."

"He doesn't live with his wife now, right?"

"No, they're separated. But whenever I've been to his place, it's been more like a frat house with his sibs and cousins around, mostly the guys. There are computers and giant TVs everywhere with video games, pool tables, and there's a setup for gambling on sports and streaming them live from around the world. You can lounge all over the place in there. There's a giant hot tub in the back with a view of the lake."

"If he doesn't live with his wife, why did he care if she inherited my mom's medallion?" I'd questioned that before and wondered if my niece knew.

Jasmine only shrugged. "Maybe he's trying to win her back."

"The lifestyle of a computer-game-addicted online gambler is sure to renew her passion for him."

I thought of our fight in the driveway. Since I'd been in wolf form for it, my memories were a little hazy, but I distinctly recalled one of his allies shooting at me with the same kind of magical silver bullet that Radomir's thugs used.

"Have you talked to his wife lately?" I asked.

"Maybe a month ago. Now that she's on her own and supporting herself, she's trying to get into selling real estate, so she talks to my mom some. She wants to specialize in leasing apartments and selling houses to those in the paranormal community. Like finding stuff that's specifically good for their unique needs."

I thought of Rue's problems and allowed that people with magical blood did have slightly different needs—or at least required more privacy—than the average human. "Are there enough paranormal people in the Seattle area moving at any given time for her to have a career?"

"I'm not sure. Do you want me to ask her next time I see her?"

"What I'd like to know is *her* opinion on my mom's medallion... and if Augustus ever said anything about trying to get it for her."

Maybe that had been a lie and he wanted it for other reasons.

"Do you think she'd be honest about it if they were scheming?" Jasmine asked.

"No, but if they're separated and *not* scheming together, she may be happy to throw him under the bus."

Jasmine looked at me.

"It's how separation works. Trust me." I looked at the time— 7:20—and sped up, following winding, tree-lined roads that led to Augustus's property. If I wanted to get there and accomplish my mission before Duncan arrived with explosives, I had to hurry.

"Up there." Jasmine pointed to a short stub of a road that veered off the main thoroughfare and down to the lake. "It's at the end. Big lot. Castle."

"It *is* a castle? I couldn't tell from the satellite imagery."

"Yup. There's a fountain in the yard with a dragon squirting water from its nostrils."

"Well, that ups the class level. I was worried by your description of the contents."

"Did you imagine Augustus living somewhere classy?"

"No. Not on a lake either. Werewolves are supposed to be into... well, not austerity necessarily, but what kind of *wolf* craves a pampered lifestyle?"

"He has a lot of money these days. He told my dad he started his own business."

"Extorting local entrepreneurs, yeah. I hear that pays well." As we rolled closer to the property, the stone walls covered with ivy hid much of the lot, but the gray stone towers of the main home—the *castle*—were visible beyond them. I wondered how many people my cousin extorted every month. To pay for this place, it had to be his full-time job. Either that, or he divvied up the extortion duties with his siblings. Given how often he'd been lurking around my apartment complex of late, it was hard to imagine him having time to personally wander all over two counties, acting like a brute while collecting payments.

I stopped the truck in front of a wrought-iron gate, a tidy green lawn and numerous sculptures visible beyond the bars. And, yes, landscaping lights shone upward onto the promised dragon fountain. The air was misty with fog creeping in from the lake. I couldn't see around the hulking castle to the dock and boathouse but thought of Duncan. If I *did* need his distraction—his help—he shouldn't have trouble getting close if he came from the water.

I eyed the lawn and tried to tell if the grass held magical security devices similar to the ones that had zapped me at Mom's cabin. I didn't sense anything similar, but we would have to be careful. Here, in his abode, Augustus had all the advantages. And I had...

"A pocket full of druidic bath bombs," I muttered.

"What?" Jasmine asked.

"Nothing."

I slipped my hand under my shirt to rub the locket Duncan and I had found together weeks earlier. A longevity talisman that had been made by a witch, it had a little power and had seemed to bolster me with energizing magic the times I'd touched it. Tonight, I could use all the help I could get.

After rubbing the locket, I pressed a button under a speaker on a cement post beside the driveway. "Pizza delivery."

"Nobody ordered a pizza," came a prompt reply.

It wasn't Augustus. Did he have a butler? *Minions*?

"Mysterious and magical wolf-case delivery," I said with an eye roll.

There was a longer pause before a panel on the post flipped down, and a camera extended out. It focused on the driver's seat, then shifted slightly to point its lens at Jasmine. After that, it lifted up on an articulating arm to peruse the rest of the truck, including the bed.

Someone was checking to see if I'd brought Duncan along.

The camera retracted, and the gate swung open.

"Guess we're invited in," I murmured.

"Looks like."

"Does he have servants?" I asked quietly as I navigated the truck inside, wondering who manned the security station.

Numerous other vehicles were parked in the large driveway in front of a four-car garage, the wooden carriage doors designed to make it look like an old-fashioned stable attached to the rest of the castle. At least there wasn't a moat filled with alligators.

"There's a cleaning service that comes every morning—Augustus can't be expected to make his own bed, you know. As far as I've seen, it's just the family that's here most of the time. That was Orazio, I think. He has an app on his phone so he doesn't have to get up to answer the gate buzzer."

"It would be tragic if he had to leave a computer game in progress."

"Tell me about it," Jasmine said. "They're all into *Destiny Wields a Sword*. I'm surprised they find the time to terrorize anyone, though Augustus doesn't play. He's the mastermind."

"That bodes well for the future of the pack."

I parked next to a Camaro with the top down. The license plate read GUSTUS. I hoped the dampness from the fog made the leather on the seats pucker.

After tucking the potions into my pockets, tissues wrapped around them to keep them from clinking, I grabbed a ski glove to wear on my left hand, gripped the case, and got out. It tingled painfully through the material, but the glove was slightly more effective than the oven mitt.

"Ready to record?" I murmured as we headed toward double wooden doors with wrought-iron bars over small windows in the tops.

As with the stone wall bordering the property, ivy crept up the sides of the castle, curling around the archway of the covered porch on its way up to the towers.

"Yup." Jasmine patted her pocket. "Is that the real artifact? I can sense magic in it."

"Unfortunately, yes." I was well aware that I risked losing it tonight. "I've tried making fake artifacts before, but they weren't that convincing. Technically, *Bolin* made my fake artifact, but I directed him."

"He has some power, doesn't he? That of a druid?"

"Yeah, but he used a 3D printer."

"I have an idea about why your artifact wasn't that convincing."

"Yup."

I lifted a finger toward the doorbell but paused, movement in the shadows of the yard catching my eye. I looked in time to spot two glowing red eyes pointed in our direction. The animal—a wolf or mongrel dog?—darted into bushes near one of the walls and disappeared from view.

"What kind of werewolf keeps guard dogs?" I muttered.

Though if Augustus had them for security, that might explain why I hadn't sensed other magical defenses.

Jasmine looked but didn't catch the eyes. I couldn't sense the animal, not the way I did most magical beings. The special water from the cave, if that was what Augustus had used, might not convey power beyond glowing eyes and an openness to obeying commands.

Another bush stirred near the side of the castle. I had a feeling there was a whole pack on the grounds. I thought about calling to warn Duncan, but there were probably cameras nestled among the ivy, and someone might be listening to us.

After bracing myself, I rang the doorbell. It sounded like a gong being struck. "That's more monastery than castle, isn't it?"

Jasmine shrugged.

The door swung open, inviting us into a stone-walled, marble-tiled foyer, with an elaborate candelabra hanging from the high ceiling.

"Does Orazio have an app for opening the door too?" I could sense werewolves deeper in the castle but none nearby.

"I think so. You can't interrupt the gaming."

"If Augustus were an organized evil overlord," I said, stepping warily inside, "we could skulk around and look for filing cabinets full of condemning paperwork, but I kind of doubt we'd find that."

"Sounds pretty old-school. People keep filing cabinets on their phones these days."

"True." Maybe I just needed to steal Augustus's *phone* to condemn him. Was Jasmine's dad enough of a computer expert to hack someone's password? I seemed to recall he programmed games, so maybe not.

We walked through the foyer and into a wide hallway, passing decorative vases and full-body suits of armor holding swords. Open doors revealed gaming rooms with the giant screens that Jasmine had promised, but nobody was lounging on the furniture. Maybe it wasn't as much of a den of laze as I'd imagined, though a hint of marijuana smoke lingered in the air, along with something that reminded me of my old alchemist's apartment. Herbs and dried flowers and magic.

After we passed a set of wide marble stairs that led upward, the hall ended in a high-ceilinged living area. It was filled with white leather couches and chairs, and arcade machines lined one wall. Toward the far end lay an open dining room and sprawling kitchen with marble countertops and fancy hanging pot racks.

All along the back wall of the castle, giant windows looked out over a manicured lawn and the lake beyond. The dock and boathouse were visible, though fog softened the view.

I tried to sense Duncan out there, but it was still more than twenty minutes until eight. It occurred to me that I would have to keep the werewolves in the castle distracted so they didn't notice his approach. He could sneak about all he wanted, but his powerful aura was hard to hide.

Landscaping lights out back shone onto a cement patio, and something moved in the shadows beyond it. A red-eyed mongrel dog. The same one we'd seen? Or another?

When Augustus stepped out of the kitchen, I jumped. Distracted by looking around, I hadn't sensed him approaching.

Two of his siblings stood behind him—they'd both been at the fight. Augustus carried an open beer can, and my heart leaped. If I could get a moment alone with it, I might be able to dump the truth elixir inside. Would the potency of the beer mask whatever the potion tasted like? And, once delivered, how long would it take to go into effect? I should have asked Rue that.

Augustus's gaze went straight to my gloved hand and the case, though he also looked at Jasmine.

"You've decided to help the betrayer?" he asked her.

"I just came along to watch," Jasmine said. "And show her how to get to your house. Did you know there are strange glowy-eyed dogs all over your yard?"

She must have seen them after all.

"I haven't betrayed anyone," I said.

My gloved fingers tightened around the case, and I wished I'd figured out more than that it had something made from metal inside. I had returned Mom's medallion before leaving her cabin, and I could have used more than vials of potions to gain the advantage over these guys. As a wolf, I could handle myself in a fight, but if I took that form, it would be hard to demand confessions or slip a potion down Augustus's throat. I had to do that as a human.

"You're the one using the pack's good name to fleece people out of money," I added.

I scratched my nose and tried to give Jasmine a significant start-recording look without being obvious. I sensed more werewolves in the kitchen or perhaps a room beyond it. My cousins. Augustus's allies.

"Wolf packs aren't supposed to have *good* names," Augustus said. "They're supposed to be strong, claim a territory that suits their needs, and woe to those who intrude upon it without asking permission. Or giving offerings. That's part of our culture and how it works."

"That only refers to other werewolves, not witches, druids, warlocks, and alchemists minding their own business and selling gas and gum from their stores."

"Did you come here to give me a lecture?" Augustus focused on the case again, his eyes barely acknowledging me.

"No. I came here for the antidote." I'd almost forgotten my ruse. It would be suspicious if I didn't demand that up front.

"How *is* your bipedfuris?" Augustus squinted at me.

"Dying."

"Where'd he come from, anyway? There supposedly aren't any werewolves left in the world that can take that form, that have that much magic."

"He's special. The antidote?"

"Let's see the box first." Augustus pointed at the case. "I heard you've been known to make fakes."

I stared at him. I'd just admitted that to Jasmine, but how would *he* know that?

My suspicious mind wanted to link Augustus to Lord Abrams and Radomir, but he might have been doing what I'd been thinking a moment ago, listening and watching us via a doorway camera.

"Why do you care about it?" Without stepping closer, I held the case up for his perusal. "I could see why you'd be interested in Mom's medallion for your wife... I guess. Do you even *talk* to her anymore?"

"That's none of your business." Augustus set the beer can down on a sofa table and walked closer, holding his hand out.

I might have given it to him if it meant I could spike his can while he was studying it, but my two other cousins stood where they would see my actions.

"It's *anti*-werewolf," I said, though I didn't quite know that, just that whatever lay inside supposedly protected against, or maybe counteracted the effects of, werewolf bites. Among other things. "It wasn't meant for you. Or any of us."

"It's *valuable*." Augustus stopped two steps away from me, his palm out expectantly.

"Where's the antidote?"

Two more of my cousins, this pair in their wolf forms, padded into view by a breakfast bar. I tensed, certain the pack was about to swarm me. And I'd gotten nothing.

"If you don't have it, I won't tell you how to get into the case," I said. "It's a box that zaps you, nothing more. The *real* power is inside."

Probably true, but I still had no idea how to open it.

"I've had someone researching its secrets," I added.

Augustus cocked an eyebrow but didn't appear that intrigued. "I don't need to know its secrets."

"You don't want what's inside for yourself then? What, are you selling it on eBay?"

He grunted. "Not eBay."

"To the guy running that potion corporation? Radomir?" Only as I said it did the answer thunk into my mind with certainty. Yes. That was the most likely explanation for where the magical silver bullets had come from.

"The market for artifacts related to werewolves, whether they're beneficial to our people or not, is hot right now."

"You don't think Radomir will pay more if you can tell him how to get into the case? I know he doesn't know. I've met him."

Augustus considered me, then pointed at Jasmine. "We don't have any beef with you. Go wait in the kitchen."

"Why?" she asked warily.

Because they were going to try to kill me and didn't want her to be hurt—or worse—in the process.

"The antidote," I stated again.

Augustus grunted in disgust but said, "Fine," and walked toward a liquor cabinet.

I turned enough to look at Jasmine while keeping Augustus in my sights. I also didn't want her to be hurt, but this might be our best opportunity.

"Do what he says," I said, then let a hand drop to my pocket where she could see it. "This isn't your fight."

While Augustus opened the cabinet door, I extracted one of the vials of truth elixir, then, moving only my eyes, glanced toward his beer can.

Jasmine caught on right away, but my other cousins were watching us.

"Okay," Jasmine said, brushing past me as she headed toward the kitchen.

I slipped the vial into her hand. She paused in front of the sofa table with the beer can, using her body to block the others' views as she uncorked it. She leaned forward as if she were interested in what Augustus would pull out of the cabinet.

There wasn't much time since he had already grabbed something. In addition to liquor bottles, there were rows of vials in racks in the cabinet, more than one glowing with magic. Nothing like a chaser of some alchemical brew to go with one's cocktail.

Jasmine dribbled the truth elixir into the beer can, wiped the top, then stuffed the empty vial into her pocket as Augustus turned back toward us.

My heart pounded. Had any of my cousins noticed? I couldn't tell, but they didn't say anything as Jasmine turned away from the sofa table and continued toward them. In fact, they ignored her completely, the men and wolves letting her pass as they took several steps into the living room. Several steps closer to me.

I licked dry lips as Augustus also walked toward me. I had to keep the conversation going longer and hope he would drink the beer. I also had to hope the truth elixir would kick in quickly.

Jasmine stopped behind the wolves, out of the way but still in view so she could record. Assuming I could get Augustus to say something...

"Here you go." He held up a vial of clear liquid that glowed faintly.

From the color alone, I knew it wasn't the antidote. Rue had *made* me the antidote, and it wasn't clear.

"Are you sure that's not a chaser for your whiskey on the rocks?"

"I'm sure." Augustus stepped closer to me, his height and broad build making him intimidating.

My skin tingled, magic trickling into my veins. My wolf blood sensed the threat and felt I needed to change. With my other cousins creeping closer, it was understandable, but I needed my human mouth to get the confession.

I eyed a suit of armor on a stand against the wall behind me.

Its empty gauntlets were wrapped around the hilt of a sword, the tip resting on the base of the stand. They gripped the weapon loosely enough that I might have been able to grab it to defend myself, but I ruefully admitted I should have brought the sword Duncan had given me if I'd wanted to do that.

"Do you already have the other wolf artifacts?" I asked Augustus.

He'd been about to grab for the case, but he paused and glanced at his allies. The wolves *and* the humans cocked their heads.

"What artifacts?" he asked.

"That's why you went to see Francisco, the *lobisomem*, right? For his South American artifacts?" I sent a silent apology to the bartender, hoping nobody harassed him because this implication got out.

"I went to *see* him because he presumed to do business near our territory without asking permission or giving an offering." Augustus stepped over to the sofa table and grabbed his beer.

It was all I could do not to hold my breath, stare at it, and will him to take a big swig. "Yeah, but he has that back room with the glowing wolf heads. You didn't sense them when you were there? Your buyer would probably be interested."

"Radomir *would* be interested," Orazio put in. "He said he'd pay for anything magical and werewolf-related that we found."

I scratched my temple to hide a glance toward Jasmine. She stood behind the others, who clearly didn't believe her a threat, and had her phone out. Camera recording? She nodded at me.

"Shut up, Orazio." Augustus drank from his beer but only a shallow swallow before glancing at it, his brow furrowing. Shit, the elixir had to have changed the taste.

Orazio snorted. "Why? She's not walking out of here alive."

I'd suspected they'd planned that, but a chill rushed through me at the naked admission.

"What the hell did you put in my beer?" Augustus threw the can at my feet, the amber liquid spattering the marble tiles.

"Why are you betraying our people and our heritage to some smarmy rich humans?" I demanded, backing toward the suit of armor.

"He's got to pay the insurance on this place," Orazio said with a short laugh. "Lake houses don't come cheap."

"Aren't you extorting enough people to pay for your ludicrous castle?" I took two more steps toward the armor.

"Give me the damn case." Augustus roared and lunged at me.

21

As Augustus lunged for me, I leaped back, spun, and snatched at the hilt of the sword held by the suit of armor. But the grip wasn't as loose as I'd hoped, and I tugged the whole statue away from the wall. Augustus reached me and threw a punch. I ducked behind the armor, and his fist clipped its metal shoulder.

"Look out, Luna," Jasmine yelled.

She'd leaped behind the breakfast bar and was eyeing a block of knives. With Augustus, two wolves, and my other two cousins charging me, that wouldn't be enough to help.

A meaty hand snatched for me—no, Augustus was trying to grab the case. I shifted farther behind the suit of armor and snaked my arm out on the other side, still trying to pull the sword free. When it didn't come, I shoved the armor at Augustus. It was heavy and crashed to the floor, but he wasn't slow enough to be caught under it.

Orazio and the wolves reached me. He grabbed my arm and yanked me away from the wall as their jaws snapped at my side. I twisted, managing to evade sharp fangs, but Augustus snatched at the case, mashing my fingers painfully as he ripped it and my glove free. He stepped away, slammed the artifact down on the sofa table, and waved at the wolves.

"End her."

Magic surged through my veins, the change coming. But with Orazio holding me and the other wolves ready to tear my throat out, the last thing I needed was to be vulnerable. And that's what I would be in those seconds before I could change.

A bang came from the kitchen, startling the men into looking. Jasmine slammed a huge stock pot down on the counter, then threw it toward my cousins.

I managed to wrest one arm free and thrust my hand into my pocket. I grabbed the first thing that my fingers brushed. One of the vials that Bolin had given me.

I threw it onto the floor between the two wolves and held my breath as I tried to lurch backward. But Orazio tightened his grip, holding me fast. As the vial shattered, green liquid spattering and vapors rising, I thrust into my pocket again. This time, I found one of the spheres I'd been calling bath bombs.

As the wolves backed away from the green haze wafting from the broken vial, their noses wrinkling, Augustus glowered at me with hatred in his eyes.

"Hold her," he barked and lunged in, fist raised to punch.

I ducked as I pulled out the sphere. His knuckles brushed my ear but missed my head. Such intense magic flowed through me that I knew the wolf was coming. I was losing the battle.

I threw the bath bomb between Augustus and Orazio, hoping it wasn't too close to my own feet. My wrist shifted in Orazio's grip. *All* of me did, my limbs and torso morphing, turning lupine.

A wolf lurching away from the vapors bumped Orazio. His grip finally loosened. I leaped away from the scrum, tearing my jacket off so I wouldn't lose all the magical items in the pockets. That was the last conscious thought—the last *human* thought—I had before I fully changed.

As I dropped to all fours, body shifting, fur sprouting, and my nose and mouth elongating into a snout, a great boom erupted outside. Yellow light flared beyond the windows, and the floor quaked under my paws.

Confusion swept through me as the wolf took over my mind. I didn't know what had caused that explosion; all I knew was that enemies were all around.

I almost sprang at the first one, the hulking human closest to me, but a powder all over the floor was turning into liquid blobs that caused the feet of the men and wolves to stick to the tiles. They almost fell over as they tried to move.

Taking advantage, I leaped in and bit a big man in the thigh.

He roared and smashed a fist toward my back. The corner of my paw stuck in one of the liquid blobs, and I almost failed to evade the blow. Pain lanced up my limb as I tore away, leaving fur and part of my paw pad attached to the tile. I rolled from the entangling mess, bumping against human furniture.

The two wolves—no, there were *three* now—ran around that furniture to avoid the sticky floors. One leaped over a wooden obstacle with a magical case on it and landed near me.

I whirled, jaws snapping for his throat. He opened his own jaws to try to reach *my* throat. Our snouts gnashed together, fangs gouging flesh, a dozen stabs of pain.

Wary of the floor, I lured the wolf back, feigning that I was afraid. When he lunged after me, his paw catching on the sticky goo, he flinched and glanced down. He pulled away, as I had, but I had time to lunge in and bite his ear. He skittered back but not before his flesh tore under my sharp teeth. Blood and fur covered my tongue. He leaped over the furniture to escape.

A shadow loomed to my side, and I dropped the chunk of ear.

Augustus had changed. Now a big dark-gray wolf, he tried to catch me off-guard, darting for my neck.

I sprang back as I turned my snout toward him to block. My fangs grazed the sensitive flesh of his nose, and he yowled in pain and fury.

Another shadow came at us from the side. I braced myself for another cousin, but it was a great bipedal creature with salt-and-pepper fur covering powerfully muscled limbs. It was one of the ancient werewolves. One who was familiar.

Duncan. Yes, we'd fought together before.

He roared and grabbed Augustus, hefting the big wolf into the air as if he weighed nothing.

As he hurled my cousins over sofas and across the room, startling silver light came from the nearby table. From the artifact. I backed away, the brilliance hurting my eyes.

But our attackers didn't stop. As Augustus crashed into furniture, the rest of my cousins charged at Duncan. They forgot me, seeing him as the more dangerous foe, the one that had to be killed before they could finish me off.

My cousins were all in wolf form now, darting in and biting for his legs and torso. I snapped at the flanks of one who came close, drawing blood. But my bites didn't deter the wolves. They were frenzied in their desire to kill the bipedfuris.

I bit my way up the flank of one foe, angling toward his throat. He twisted, dodging a swipe from Duncan, and I caught his shoulder instead. Hoping to deter a counterattack, I sank my teeth in deep.

The wolf jerked his head toward me, fangs gleaming with saliva in the silver light. Not backing away, I sank my fangs deeper and shook, trying to knock him off his feet. The wolf stumbled, and Duncan caught him with a clawed hand, a powerful blow that knocked our enemy several feet. The wolf slammed into a wall, leaving blood.

As Duncan whirled toward another attacker, something clattered behind me. The suit of armor fell to the floor, the pieces flying away. A naked human lunged in and grabbed the sword from the mess. Augustus. His wolf magic had left him.

"Pin him down!" he yelled to his allies as he ran toward Duncan with the sword raised.

Something oily smeared the blade, something my human eyes hadn't been keen enough to notice. Fear for Duncan surged through me, the certainty that he was in trouble. And his back was to Augustus as he dealt with two wolves.

I charged at my cousin, intending to knock him from his trajectory. I clipped him, knocking him into a sofa, but I'd forgotten about the sticky floors. One of my paws caught.

Augustus spun toward me, sweeping at my head with the sword. I ducked, almost losing an ear of my own as it whistled through the air above me. With a great yank, I pulled my paw free and lunged around the mess on the floor to knock Augustus back. He stumbled, almost losing his grip on the weapon.

With a roar, Duncan batted aside his attackers and turned toward Augustus. Again, I lunged for my cousin, but he saw Duncan facing us with arms spread and legs crouched, about to spring. Augustus startled me by hurling the sword at Duncan. The bipedfuris wasn't as fast and agile as a wolf. He might yet have dodged the weapon, but, at the same time, one of my cousins rammed into him from behind. The blade sliced into the furry flesh of Duncan's side, sinking deep enough to spill blood.

Fury roared through my veins, the most savage of my instincts rising and taking over. As had happened before, I lost all rational thought. All I knew was that I had to slay the one who'd attacked he who I wanted to be my mate.

Driven by crazed frenzy, I charged into Augustus, jaws gnashing wildly. A dozen times I bit, drawing blood, gouging deep into vulnerable flesh. Augustus managed to punch me, but I didn't feel it.

A clunk sounded nearby, another ally striking a wolf with a pot, keeping him from reaching me. Relentless, I tore into the enemy before me. Augustus tried to run, but the furniture impeded him, and his foot caught on the floor. He pitched to his knees, leaving his throat at the level of my snout. Without hesitation, without mercy, I lunged in and ended his life.

22

AFTER AUGUSTUS FELL, THE REST OF MY ENEMIES FLED, MOST limping and leaving blood on the floors. My awareness returned slowly, along with the knowledge that Duncan had been injured.

His magic faded before mine, leaving him naked and human on his back, his hand to his side, blood leaking through his fingers. I'd seen him injured a dozen times, and most wounds he shrugged off, trusting his regenerative werewolf magic to heal him. But something was different this time. I could see it in his stricken face, the uncharacteristic fear in his eyes.

I whined uncertainly, coming close to sniff his wound. That was when I detected it, something off, something mingling with the blood. I remembered the oily gleam on the sword.

What had coated it? Venom? Like from a rattlesnake? Or poison made by humans?

"My heart is flopping around in my chest like a dying fish," Duncan whispered, touching my jaw. "Is he dead?"

Yes, Augustus was, but I couldn't say that as a wolf. And I couldn't help Duncan in this form.

Adrenaline still pumped through my veins, but I willed the

magic to fade, for my humanity to return. I couldn't remember what, but there was something I could do to help him as a human.

The magic disappeared, leaving me on my knees at Duncan's side. His hand shifted from his wound to his heart. Right away, I remembered what I had that might help. I shoved myself to my feet, stepped over my cousin's body, and delved into my jacket pockets, glad I'd cast that aside before changing. I'd thrown Bolin's sphere, but most of the vials remained inside. I dug out one of the antidotes.

But would it do anything for this particular poison? As I knelt again by Duncan, I realized this had to be something different from the one Augustus had mixed into the chocolate. That had been slow-acting, designed to make it hard to pin down what caused a death. But this... This was killing Duncan quickly.

"Drink this," I whispered, hoping it would somehow work anyway.

Fingers shaking with fear that it wouldn't be enough, I lifted Duncan's head and held the vial to his lips.

"Smells awful," he whispered but didn't object to me draining it into his mouth.

"All good medicine does."

The potion slid down his throat, but the worried look in his eyes didn't leave, the fear of impending death. I rested two fingers on his neck and felt his erratic pulse. With my own fear increasing, I grabbed another vial and spattered it over his wound, on the off chance that might help.

"Is that... hygienic?" Duncan whispered, managing a fleeting smile.

"No, but if you die, it won't matter if it gets infected."

"Comforting."

I rested a hand on his abdomen, looking around for something more I could do. If Augustus kept poisoned swords in his house, might there be an antidote around? Could one of the vials in the medicine cabinet be the cure?

I rose, thinking to check and hope for labels, but Duncan caught my wrist.

"Don't go," he whispered.

"I need to look for an antidote. I don't think what I gave you was the right one for that poison."

"I've lived almost my whole life alone," Duncan said. "I'm realizing... very late... that I don't want to die alone."

His face was pale, his fingers blue-tinged. The erratic heartbeats weren't pumping enough blood through his body.

With a lump in my throat, I whispered, "I don't want you to die at all. I need to find something."

"Uhm, Aunt Luna?" came Jasmine's voice from the kitchen.

She held her phone, probably indicating she'd recorded at least some of the altercation, but that was the least of my worries at that moment.

"Is that... your case?" Jasmine pointed at the sofa table, at a silver glow coming from the top.

"Oh," I blurted, reminded that it had started glowing during the fight.

No, more than that. The case had *opened*.

What had prompted that I didn't know, but the translation of the words inscribed on the bottom came to mind: *Straight from the source lies within protection from venom, poison, and the bite of the werewolf.*

"I'm not leaving, just grabbing that," I told Duncan so he would release my wrist. Even dying and in his mere human form, he was strong.

Maybe he saw the glow because he let go without questioning me further.

I lunged for the table. With the lid back, the case's glow was so great that I couldn't see what lay inside. Expecting it to zap the hell out of me, I reached in anyway. There was no time to hunt for my glove.

The metallic object inside was warm to the touch, but it didn't zap me when I pulled it out. It *did* tingle against my palm, emanating magic that crackled in the air around me. Since it was the source of the glow, the case grew dark afterward, save for the reflection of light against its mother-of-pearl interior. The item itself felt like it had a handle and a top. With no idea how it worked, I knelt beside Duncan again.

"I'm going to..." I trailed off as the strong urge to set the item on Duncan's chest came to me. Was it my idea or was the artifact suggesting it?

I didn't know, but Duncan's eyes had closed, his hand dropping from his chest to his side, and I worried he might already have passed. I rested the object on his chest, hoping it would somehow know what to do and have the power to save a life.

Silver light flashed, almost blinding me. Even as I squinted and looked away, I saw a dark silhouette in the brilliance. It was... mushroom-shaped? If so, I'd been grabbing a stem rather than a handle, but the metallic element promised it wasn't some preserved fungal fossil from nature.

Despite its blinding effects, I kept it on Duncan's chest. Power radiated up my arm but also flowed into his body via tendrils of magical energy that spread all over him. Like mycelium, I thought. If the artifact had been based on mushrooms, maybe that made sense.

Light also flowed out of it and intensified around the wound in Duncan's side. That gave me hope that it knew what it was doing, that it *could* help.

"Should I be recording this?" Jasmine asked uncertainly.

"Can you see anything but brilliant light?"

"Not really."

"Let's just wait and see what—" The light intensified like a solar flare—or a nuclear bomb detonating. It filled every nook in the room, if not the house, and probably blinded people on the other side of the lake.

Duncan gasped, his back arching. I put my hand back on his chest, fresh fear and distress filling me. What if the artifact killed him instead of healing him?

The light disappeared, leaving me blinking and struggling to see in the abrupt return to normal.

Duncan took another breath, this one less distressed, then another. After a moment, he blinked and opened his eyes. "Luna?"

My vision starting to recover, I looked down at him. The wound hadn't healed entirely, but it had stopped bleeding and scabbed over, now looking like it was days instead of minutes old. In my human form, I couldn't tell if it smelled of a foreign substance, but it looked better. *Duncan* looked better, color returning to his face.

"I'm here." I patted his abdomen.

"Fondling my torso, yes." He sounded agreeable—and much better than he had a couple of minutes ago.

"I put a strange glowing mushroom on it, so I thought you deserved a little fondling."

"I *usually* do, but..." His brows rose as he dipped his chin to look at the artifact. "A mushroom?"

"Well, it's mushroom-*shaped*. It's obviously... something else. Not a key, though, I don't think. Your dream of unlocking dragon-guarded treasure with it may go unfulfilled."

"Did it... save my life?"

"Yeah. I think it nullified the poison and... more." I waved to his quickly healing wound. "It has some powerful magic."

"I'll say." Duncan's hand drifted to his heart. "I was sure I was going to die."

"I worried about that too."

He turned his head left and right, looking around the room,

his gaze lingering on Augustus's body but only momentarily. He eyed the table and the case. I could still sense magic from it, but much greater magic emanated from the artifact on Duncan's chest. The case had to be insulated, dulling magic so that its hidden treasure hadn't been that noticeable. Had it been, I would have sensed it in the duct under my bedroom floor long before Duncan had come along with his magic detector. Even with my powers quashed by that potion, I wouldn't have missed this thing.

"How did you open the box?" Duncan picked up the artifact.

It pulsed twice, and he hurried to set it on the floor. Even though it had saved his life, he wasn't presuming it was friendly. I wouldn't either.

"I..." I started to say that I didn't know, but the timing of when the case had opened couldn't have been a coincidence. "I think *you* did."

Duncan touched his chest, eyebrows rising again.

"It was when you ran in here as the bipedfuris. The thing started glowing like a sun. I think that's when the lid opened."

"That's surprising, especially given that inscription. It's *anti-*werewolf, right? It shouldn't respond to me in any way, to any werewolf."

I held up a finger. "Actually, this may make sense. It could be the presence of a werewolf that releases the artifact. Presumably, whoever owns it might need it if one of our kind showed up, right? Like if you were to bite some innocent druid, the druid would need to promptly be healed before the lycanthrope magic could take hold in his or her blood."

"So, you think it's the presence of a threat that releases the lid? That's interesting. Would *any* threat do?"

"Maybe any of the ones it's supposed to protect against. Were-wolf bites, venom, and poison."

"Under that logic, waving a rattlesnake at the case might also cause the lid to open." Duncan sat up and looked around, as if one might be lurking in the room so we could use it for a test.

"Rattlesnakes are hard to come by in western Washington."

"Oh? I suppose they aren't into the damp climate."

"Nope. Even in eastern Washington, where it's drier, you're not going to find them in winter."

"Are there any scorpions here?"

"Sorry, no. You'll have to go to Arizona for those."

"Are there *no* venomous beasties in the Seattle area?"

"No, it's a venom-free paradise. That's why we put up with the rain. I—"

Baying came from outside the castle—or was that *inside* the castle?—and I stopped short. When the rest of my cousins had fled, I hadn't expected them to return, but I remembered the glowing-eyed mongrels. My cousins might have stuck around and rounded them up, then waited until they sensed that the biped-furis magic had faded, that Duncan and I were human again.

A bang sounded, the front door slamming open. The loud bays of the mongrels echoed through the castle halls.

I groaned. I hadn't been seriously injured, not the way Duncan had, but the thought of fighting again was exhausting.

Duncan pushed himself to his feet. "You two, go out the back."

"Not without you," I said.

"I'll buy you time to get away. Take the artifact and the case and get them out of here. They're even more powerful—more important—than we thought."

"You almost *died* two minutes ago. You can't—"

"I'm fine. My boat is tied up at the property line. You can take it and get away until it's safe to come back." Duncan grabbed the artifact, put it in the case, closed the lid, and handed it to me. His eyelids drooped as feral power radiated from him. "I'm feeling vigorous after that healing. I'll keep them from chasing after you."

"Why don't we *all* go?" Jasmine suggested.

She'd no sooner said the words than the first glowing-eyed mongrel ran into view, claws clacking on the marble tiles. Barks and yips came from the hallway behind it, promising more on its heels. Its eyes locked on me.

"Go." Duncan grabbed the fallen sword and stepped into the path of the guard dogs while waving me toward a door to the patio.

Hating the idea of leaving him, I wanted to stay, to grab a knife from the kitchen and help. But Jasmine was obeying Duncan, running out the door to the patio. She didn't have a weapon. If there were more red-eyed guard dogs out there, she might need help.

"Just buy us a couple of seconds, and come right after," I called to Duncan as I took the case and ran after Jasmine.

He grunted as an answer, swinging the sword to keep the dogs at bay. Red eyes flashed as they turned toward me. Whoever was left in charge must have told them to go after me specifically.

"Of course," I muttered, running across the patio and into the yard.

As I trailed Jasmine down a path toward the water, I sensed Duncan's aura fluctuate in the castle behind us. Was he turning into the bipedfuris again? Since I couldn't change into a wolf two times close together, his ability to do so surprised me, but maybe he felt he would keep the dogs at bay more effectively in that form.

Jasmine reached the boat first, finding it among reeds near the destroyed dock, and pushed it into the water. It was an open motorboat, and I jumped in after her. Roars and barks came from the house as we floated into the lake. She started the motor and, with the experience of someone who'd done it before, navigated us out into the water.

"Let's wait for him," I said when we were twenty or thirty feet from shore, boards from the destroyed dock bumping against the hull of the boat.

Magic pricked at my skin. Familiar magic that I'd felt before. The last time it had whispered past me, Duncan had been pulled away, up to the north to those who wanted to use him once more.

A boom came from the house, and orange flashed behind the windows, blowing several out. Another of Duncan's explosives? Did he have the wherewithal to detonate them while in the biped-furis form? It was hard to imagine. Maybe one of my cousins had charged in with grenades.

"This is chaos," Jasmine whispered, taking her phone out and recording, though we couldn't see much of the fight from the lake. We *could* see fire burning inside the house now.

"Tell me about it. How much did you get recorded before?"

Wood snapped in the castle. A beam breaking and falling? I willed Duncan to come out, to leave the mongrels behind and join us.

"It's mostly audio since my phone was in my pocket anytime someone was looking at me, but I got Augustus and some of the others talking about selling the artifacts."

"Okay, good."

Numbness crept into my limbs as the fact that I'd killed Augustus sank in. What would the rest of the pack think? Would they understand or swear vengeance on me? I hadn't intended to kill him. I'd never wanted that.

In the castle, the barks and roars died down, leaving only the crackle of fires burning. Movement in the yard drew my eye. I expected one of the red-eyed guard dogs, but a furry figure on two legs loped across the lawn.

I lifted an arm, hoping to wave Duncan toward us, but he didn't look in our direction. The magic that beckoned him whispered past me again, raising the hair on the back of my neck.

"Duncan!" I called as loudly as I dared. "Fight it! Stay here!"

His head didn't turn in my direction. Drawn by his creator's power, the bipedfuris leaped over hedges and the stone wall surrounding the property. Soon, he disappeared into the night.

I slumped down in the boat. No red-eyed animals ran out of the castle to attack us now that Duncan was gone. Maybe he'd taken care of them before letting himself be drawn away.

Sirens wailed in the distance.

"Where to?" Jasmine asked.

"Not far." I waved to a neighbor's dock. "I need to circle back and get my truck. Ideally before the firefighters and police and whoever else arrive." Reminded that I was naked, I hurried to put my jacket on, checking my pockets for the truck keys.

"Okay." Jasmine navigated the boat along the shoreline. "Is he, uhm, going to come back?"

"I don't know."

"At least you and I survived the night, and Augustus..." Jasmine looked toward the smoking mess of the castle. "Well, he won't keep trying to kill you."

"One small boon," I murmured.

"I'll show the footage to Lorenzo and the arbiter and everyone. Then they'll know... Well, they'll just know."

We hadn't gotten the detailed confession that I'd hoped for, but I thought what Augustus and Orazio had revealed would be enough. They'd been doing even more vile stuff than I'd realized, not only bullying the paranormal beings of the Seattle area but helping artifact thieves steal from their own people. Even if Augustus hadn't been behind the attack at Mom's cabin, he'd been colluding with those who had been. The elders would agree that his end had been warranted, and they might force his siblings out of the pack too.

I should have been happy, or at least relieved, but as I gazed off to the north, I felt like more uncertainties than certainties remained.

"Yes," I said, aware of Jasmine watching me. Maybe she also

felt uncertain and hoped for reassurance. "Thank you for your help."

"You're welcome. You're a really badass wolf, you know."

Badass was the last thing I felt in that moment, but I said another, "Thank you," as we turned for a dock.

With weariness settling over my body, along with the pain and awareness of all my injuries, my only remaining goal for the night was to retrieve my truck and go home.

EPILOGUE

IN THE TWENTY-ODD YEARS I'D BEEN THE PROPERTY MANAGER AT Sylvan Serenity Housing, I'd never helped anyone move into the complex. Happy to save my employers money, I did a lot of extra jobs, but I drew the line at toting in people's TVs, computers, and boxes. That had been the case until today, anyway. Rue had arrived, her only assistant a gangly, geeky grandson two inches shorter and ten pounds lighter than me. It was possible he'd needed a phone book to sit on to drive the moving truck up from Seattle for her.

As soon as she'd spotted me, Rue had put me to work. Admittedly, I'd been lurking near the parking lot, ostensibly raking and tidying the landscaping but hoping to see a familiar Roadtrek roll in.

It had been three days since my showdown with my cousins, and, despite trying to call his number numerous times, I hadn't heard from Duncan since he'd disappeared in his bipedfuris form. Was he once again wounded and in a ditch? Had his creator decided he was too much trouble and killed him? Had Radomir chained him up to use whenever he needed muscles that weren't amped up on potions?

I didn't know, but I missed him. I'd been on the verge of driving up to that potion factory to see if he needed rescuing, but one of my half-siblings had arrived to collect me. The day after Augustus's death, the pack had started the first of three meetings to determine the fate of my remaining cousins, and I'd been needed to present my evidence and answer questions.

During the meetings, the arbiter, Lorenzo, and numerous elders had reviewed Jasmine's footage of the confrontation at the lake house. At some point, Jasmine had also gone to Francisco, the store owners, and the leader of a witch coven to get video testimonials describing Augustus and saying how much money he'd extorted out of them over the last year.

The elders had been difficult to read as they'd watched the videos. None of them had looked fondly in my direction. Augustus might have been the most vocal person about voicing disdain for the years I'd abandoned the pack—and taken that potion—but the vibe from others suggested many felt I wasn't to be trusted. I wished they knew I'd risked my life to get Mom's medallion back and help the pack, but she'd kept its theft close to her chest, so few people knew it had ever been stolen. At least the elders hadn't scoffed or been dismissive when presented with the evidence.

Also, nobody had suggested I should be punished or exiled for killing a relative. Werewolves didn't do that, not unless foul play was involved. The pack knew Augustus had challenged me numerous times, and nobody seemed surprised by his death. Only his siblings—and colleagues in the mafia gig they'd been running —had glared balefully at me. But their association with Augustus and the artifact thieves had gotten them in trouble. In the end, the elders had banished several of my cousins. I hoped they *stayed* banished and that I wouldn't see them again.

It had been a victory, even if I hadn't intended Augustus's death. Too bad I didn't have someone to celebrate it with. Instead, I was carrying boxes of alchemy equipment and incense in the rain, the latter potent even through the cardboard, and I kept sneezing.

"Ah yes," Rue said, waving me in. "That is the last box. Place it there. Perfect."

"Glad I could help," I said dryly.

I might have said no, but she *had* made potions for me.

"Already, I am enjoying this domicile. There is a *tree* outside my window instead of honking traffic. Isn't that fabulous?"

"I didn't know alchemists enjoy nature, but I'm glad it's acceptable."

"Yes. It will keep nosy snoops from peering in, monitoring my work, and jumping to conclusions about the potions I'm brewing."

"Was that a big problem in the Seattle high-rise? It looked like your windows all faced the building across the street, not any of your neighbors."

"The denizens in the building across the street *spoke* to my neighbors. They are the ones who first started the gossip. One of them even kept a telescope on his balcony. For watching the *stars*, he told the police when I complained, but he used it to peer into other people's homes. He was a pervert."

"I think I would make that assumption too. Between the light pollution and the cloud cover, Seattle isn't exactly an astronomer's dream."

"No, they use their tools to spy on their nude neighbors instead. *Perverts.*" Rue dug into her pocket. "I will tip you for your service."

"That's not necessary."

Instead of money, she pulled out a little bag that clinked. "These are beauty and longevity potions. You'll find the wrinkle cream perfect for your fine lines." Rue peered at my face. "And that forehead crease that is not so fine. Have you been sleeping?"

"Not nearly enough."

"Definitely use the wrinkle cream. I do every night before bed, and you can see the youthful smoothness of my face."

"It looks very nice."

"Yes."

In the hope that I would see Duncan again, I accepted the bag, willing to try alchemically enhanced wrinkle cream. It probably worked better than the hyaluronic-acid gunk I smeared on my face at night. I still found it laughable that Mom thought I was of an age that having children would be a good idea. Though I admitted that my perimenopause symptoms had lessened of late. It was possible I'd simply been too busy to notice them, but... maybe my wolf magic was helping keep my body in homeostasis now that I'd stopped taking the potion that sublimated it. Fine lines aside, I'd been sleeping better—when I could actually get home at a reasonable time to engage in it.

After leaving Rue's apartment, I was heading back to my own when a tenant with a clogged toilet waylaid me. My life continued to be glamourous. At least it was an easy fix, and I finished by the time an SUV with a Millennium Falcon sticker on the back of one of the side mirrors rolled into the parking lot. I'd seen it before but not for months. It belonged to Austin's friend, the one who'd been picking him up from the airport. I lifted a hand and waved, then jogged over as the passenger-side door opened.

Austin grinned as he stepped out, brown hair painfully short in a military buzz cut. It made his ears look bigger than usual, but he still managed to be handsome.

"Hey, Mom." He spread his arms to let me hug him fiercely, then patted my back in a tolerating manner. Neither of my sons had ever been the touchy-feely types, but they endured embraces from their mother.

I let Austin grab a duffel bag out of the car and thank his friend before gripping his arms to look him up and down. He'd lost a few pounds, his face leaner than when he'd left, though baggy cargo pants and a hoodie made him look more like a college student than a soldier, and was that mustard on his sleeve? It must have been a long trip.

"I imagined you arriving home all respectable and dashing in a uniform," I said, though I supposed I wouldn't fly in such a thing if it weren't required.

"My dress blues are in my duffel. I imagined *you* washing and ironing them for me before I go back." He grinned wider.

"The Air Force hasn't matured you as much as I envisioned."

"It's only been six months."

"Will it be another six before you learn to do your own laundry?"

"Maybe nine. I did bring you a Christmas present. Maturely." Austin patted the duffel.

"Did you buy it at one of the overpriced gift shops in the airport?"

"Well... you're stuck on base most of the time when you're in training. There weren't many opportunities to shop."

"That's a yes. That's okay. I'm glad you're here to visit." I didn't mention that his brother's only response to the message I'd left, wishing him happy holidays and asking if he needed anything, had been a gif of a cat batting Christmas-tree ornaments. Maybe someday Cameron would get over his grudge and want to have a relationship with his mother again. I hoped so.

"For more than a week, yup. Ozzie still lives here, right?" Austin waved across the complex toward the building where one of his friends who was a year younger and a senior in high school resided.

"Yes, and he and his mom, against the lease, still have three dogs, four cats, parakeets, and a ferret. Based on the pet-food bags

I've seen go into that apartment, there might be multiple ferrets there by now."

"I'm sure his mom appreciates you keeping tabs on them."

"I have no doubt. Are you going to visit?"

"Do you mind? I need to check on a bet we made. He might owe me money. Then I'll come home for dinner."

I decided to pretend Austin had come to see me as much as he had his friends. All I said was, "It's breakfast-for-supper. Bacon and eggs."

Thanks to Duncan's shopping trip, I had lots of both.

"Perfect." Austin left his duffel bag on the damp walkway and jogged toward his friend's apartment. Whatever he'd gotten me at the gift shop must not have been prone to water damage.

I picked up the duffel, hefted it over my shoulder, and headed toward my apartment.

Austin noticed and halted. "Mom, you don't have to carry that. I'll come back for it."

"I don't want my gift stolen." I decided not to mention the increased crime in the area. That was still a problem that I needed to deal with, or at least that the local business owners *wished* I would deal with. I doubted Augustus had been doing anything to squelch it, so I didn't anticipate it getting worse, but having him gone wouldn't improve things either.

"It's heavy," Austin warned.

"It's fine."

It wasn't any worse than Rue's boxes of potions, tools, and ingredients.

Austin eyed the duffel over my shoulder, seeming to debate between grabbing it or running off to see his friend. Ultimately, he trotted back over, took it from me, and we headed toward the apartment together.

"I'll put it away first," he said.

"It's nice that the military has taught you some manners."

"You'll be more inclined to do my laundry if your back isn't thrown out."

"That is true."

"Though your back seems fine." Austin gave me a sidelong look. "I think I'm losing my bet with Ozzie."

"It involves me?"

"And how many toilets, in the time I was gone, he would see you carrying out of the parking lot while he was doing homework at his computer. I figured that since me and Cameron are all grown and gone, you'd take it easy. Maybe get an assistant to help out here. Or a real handyman. Then you could take up knitting or something."

"I'm forty-five, not eighty-five."

The confused look he gave me suggested that there wasn't, in the eyes of an eighteen-year-old, much difference.

"And I can still carry a toilet," I said.

"How *many* did you carry? More than five?"

"Is that part of the bet?"

"Maybe."

"You're kind of a weirdo, my son."

"I think that's inherited."

"I believe that's true."

Once in our apartment, Austin tossed his duffel bag on the bottom bunk in his bedroom, which, other than dusting and sweeping, I hadn't touched while he'd been gone. Then, he managed to ask how work was, say the property looked like it was in good shape, and praise the presence of the espresso maker, since mess-hall coffee was apparently gross.

"Oh, let me get your present. You may want to eat it now instead of waiting for Christmas morning." He smirked mischievously at me, ducked back into his room, and rummaged in his duffel before returning.

I waited curiously to see what edible fare he'd brought, courtesy of whatever airport he'd flown through on the way home from Mississippi.

"Here you go. Exotic chocolate. You'll love it."

"Oh? I didn't know the South was known for exotic chocolate."

Austin extended a tin clumsily wrapped in tissue paper and secured with enough tape that I almost needed to change into a wolf and use my fangs to open it. Since my sons didn't know about that secret, I opted for scissors instead.

"I'm not sure it is, but they have a lot of big insects," he said as I revealed what looked like a cricket on the front of the tin. "Since you love chocolate with bacon bits in it, I figured this would be in the same category."

I looked dubiously at the offering. "Austin, I know you're young and inexperienced in the ways of the world, but there's no realm in which bacon and crickets are in the same category."

"You're going to try it anyway, though, right? I've never seen you turn your nose up at protein. Even *crunchy* protein."

"I... suppose I might."

If Duncan returned, I would share the gift with him.

Austin glanced at a text on his phone. Probably feeling he'd fulfilled his duties as a visiting son, he promised to return later and bolted off to visit his friend.

Though I was left alone in the apartment, it felt less empty, at least for the time being. I found myself looking around and missing Duncan's company though. If he didn't call or show up by morning, I would drive up to look for him.

My gaze landed on the sword he'd given me. I thought about tucking it into my bedroom closet so Austin wouldn't wonder why I had acquired such a thing. But I considered the crime problem and wondered if the Sylvans would drop their interest in selling the complex if someone addressed that issue. I also thought of how little fighting expertise I had when I wasn't in my wolf form. Duncan was right. It wouldn't be a bad idea to learn to use the blade. Augustus might be gone, but I highly doubted my problems were over.

I took out my phone and tapped in *sword-fighting lessons*, vowing to sign up somewhere after the holidays.

THE END